T0102931

From Defeat To Victory

From Defeat To Victory

Destiny at Any Cost

Anna James

authorHOUSE®

AuthorHouse™
1663 Liberty Drive
Bloomington, IN 47403
www.authorhouse.com
Phone: 1 (800) 839-8640

Published by AuthorHouse 07/30/2015

ISBN: 978-1-5049-2069-8 (sc)
ISBN: 978-1-5049-2068-1 (e)

Print information available on the last page.

This book is printed on acid-free paper.

Contents

ACKNOWLEDGEMENT

Praise the Lord! It is with a humble heart that I salute my Lord and Savior Jesus Christ who is the head of my life. Thank you for being my guide all the way; without you none of this would have been possible. I would also like to thank God for my family and friends who were a blessing and strong support on this journey. To my beautiful and supportive mother, Melva Williams who literally provided the resources to launch this project, thank you mommy, I love you. To my Bishop Leslie Josiah Barnes who blessed me and sent me fort as I choose this route. I am humbled and honored to have a true father in the gospel. To Darnett Cohen-Spencer my senior director and sister in Christ, I love you. You were my angel in the flesh in my most dire need, thank you for keeping me in check when I wanted to give up in my affliction. To my brother-in-law Duane Johnson, who was my unofficial doctor when I was going through the storm and my feet felt lifeless. To my precious Aunt and spiritual mother Aileen James, you are a woman of wisdom and patience, you listened to my crying and laugher and I was strengthened in due season. To my most precious jewel Destiny who has been my source of strength and joy, I love you my miracle child; thanks for being my greatest fan. To my two beautiful and blessed sisters, Harriet and Chudey and my BFF Paulette, you guys are my inspiration, you have loved me even when I was unlovable; you guys are irreplaceable.

To the women's department of First United Church of Jesus Christ Apostolic, with the leading of President Jennifer Bennett that blessed me with an award for mother's day 2007; you planted a seed by presenting me the life changing book from Bishop T.D Jakes entitled 'Reposition Yourself". To my dear children Jelane and Ashley who despite many anguish, secretly gave me the strength to never give up, knowing that I had to let them realize that my God is greater than every storm. To my newest friend and sister in the Lord Sister Andrea Mcleod who quoted to me "2015 means this is it, this is your year for change"; thank you woman of God. To my faithful brother and friend Michael Fraser who unselfishly shared his mentor, Pastor Tai with me, who told me "within you is a story, go ahead and tell it". To Pastor Heston Williams and his beautiful wife Sharese Williams, thank you for being a silent source of strength; I love you guys so much.

In closing special thanks to Sister Charlene Vernon who showed up at my door and motivated me to get what the Lord had for me; I am so thankful for your charity. To Bishop Wayne Brown from London England who saw the gift and believed enough to fight for me in the spirit; that was priceless. To God be all the glory for you. To my anointed and powerful spiritual children Peter, Christina, Klonde and Joey, you guys have given me a reason to live and press on to the mark of the high calling; thank you.

In closing I want to thank my greatest fans and motivators. I saved the best for last, my favorite nephew Onhoj Daniel Johnson and his beautiful little sister Tierrah Kylee Johnson. These guys kept me on point and cheered me on along the way. The "Yeah Team", I love you with all my heart; you guys typed and research and did so much without a murmur, God bless you forever!

FOREWORD

Onyumalechi James also lovingly known as Anna, is gifted in the area of exercising faith and has expressed to those who know her that "without faith it is impossible to please God". She has been a vibrant and expressive writer since childhood and this gift is superbly displayed in this, her introductory novel from the "Defeat to Victory" series. Onyumalechi handwrote her first novel in her early teen years but never had it published. I read that book and knew deep within my spirit that one day my loving sister would be a trailblazer in this arena. She is a talented and focused woman of God who is determined to be a spiritual shepherd to millions around the globe through prayer and fasting. In January 2007 she started the Ephesians 4 prayer line and through this ministry proved to be an altruistic philanthropist in her native island, Jamaica.

Onyumalechi is a God-sent, fueled by a passion to fulfill God's mandate for these turbulent times through her writing. She has a zeal for those in Christendom who struggle with faith. She has been tried, tested and has proved that the Lord hears and answers prayers of those who trust and believe by faith. She is an exemplary individual who trusts in the Lord with all her heart, knowing that He is God. She is grateful to the Lord Jesus who has touched her superbly through divine healing. She has a gift of merging spirituality with everyday living which naturally provokes her mentees and spiritual children to pursue a life of integrity.

In this novel, she focused on a young man called David who despite the odds, held on in faith to the Almighty God. Should he throw in the towel? Or even lament on the situation he dealt with from childhood? Maybe yes! This is a page turner that takes you on a journey of determination, character, blessings and favor of a humble lad. Each chapter ignites a desire for the next and truly every reader can relate to this story. Throughout the journey of preparing for this novel, Anna would profusely sweat at times but was determined to complete this life changing novel that readers will not regret reading.

Harriet James-Johnson
Educational Program Administrator
Brooklyn, New York.

Introduction

He had to remind himself that the worst years were behind him. Almost a man now at the age of seventeen, he took on a stature comprised of masculine good looks with the flawless countenance of an angel. He was caramel in tone, and his hair beautifully contoured naturally at his nape. He stood 6 feet in height, not completely bulging in masculinity but good enough to hold his own. His attractive features did not take him to a place of conceit. With all his good looks and structure, he was full of humility and honor. He continued to walk toward his first destination and realized that the presence of God was thick round about him; he began to see the glory of his God. He realized the splendor of grass before him; how brisk the wind was and how sweetly the birds sang. It was truly a fact that all of nature had joined him in worship; one must truly realize that the anointed one is ever present.

Chapter 1

It was the break of day and David knew he hadn't had enough sleep, but that was not of relevance to him; sleep was not a priority on his agenda. His expectations exceeded his basic priority. His nights were usually ones of restless proportion but this had become the norm to him; however he does his best to put his best face forward to perform what was expected of him. It was now 5am, the morning was still but his day was already fully matured. He arose from his place of rest and began to fold his worn out linen that kept him slightly warm due to the tattered conditions they had become after being used overtime. He made his way toward a broken washroom which was his daily routine. The time was far spent; fifteen minutes had passed since he arose. With a smile on his face and joy in his heart, the thought of knowing that his Shepherd, his Father, his Friend had graced him to see yet another day where mercy was shown toward him yet again. David mentally prepared for the daily tasks set before him. His shower was not as lengthy as he would have liked. With praise, he went before his God and in spirit he began to worship. He closed out the world and his cares that were set around him; touching the heavens in sincerity of his heart and bowing in reverence to the Most High One. It was a hard knock of disturbance that brought him back to reality and the voice on the exterior spoke, 'we leave in half an hour'. With less enthusiasm, he closed out his time of intimacy as was his custom by repeating the psalm, 'the Lord is my Shepherd I shall not want'.

The day was unexpectedly feeling like that of springtime even though it was the margin of winter. This made him very happy as his coat was less than perfect and his boots could do with a little more inside padding. As he walked toward the main house, his countenance fell, but he began to encourage himself, as this has now become his norm, 'Just keep smiling in the Lord'. He had to remind himself that the worst years were behind him. Almost a man, now at the age of seventeen he took on a stature comprised of masculine good looks with the flawless countenance of an angel. He was caramel in tone, and his hair beautifully contoured naturally at his nape. Standing at 6 feet, not completely bulging in masculinity but good enough to hold his own. His attractive features did not take him to a place of conceit. With all his good looks and structure, he was full of humility and honor. He continued to walk toward his first destination but realized that the presence of God was thick round about him; he began to see the glory of His God and realized how beautiful the splendor of grass was before him. How brisk the wind was and how sweetly the bird sang. It was truly a fact that all of nature had joined him in worship. One truly must realize that the anointed one is ever present. You will never have to look too far to find him. David opened a gate that led him to the entrance of the property and proceeded to wait for his departure to his job site. It must have been about an hour, but to him it seemed like minutes. This was so because the joy of the Lord was his strength and in Him was sweet serenity.

Lost in thought he was awakened to reality when a sweet musical like sound ringed his name. "Hi son", said Ma Anna, the maid of the great house, who was more like a mother to him. She held his face in maternal embrace and recited her daily question, "how was your sleep"? His reply was always the same, "my sleep was sweet Ma Anna". She chuckled and replied, "our Lord is watching over his beloved". In her heart, she wished his mom could see him now but circumstances beyond her control brutally separated mother and child immediately after he was weaned. This pained Ma Anna and she prayed daily that Joy and her baby would one day be reunited. She spoke to Joy daily in the spirit and prayed that she forgave herself as God had forgiven her. She then handed him a bag of warm edibles which consists also of a golden apple and a soft muffin. He thanked her and spoke in a voice full of gratitude saying, "Ma Anna, I don't know what I would have done hadn't the Lord given you that heart of compassion and the kindness you show toward me". "You're welcome my son", Ma Anna replied choking back the tears from resounding in the atmosphere. "I thank the Lord for His grace towards me. You're the son the Lord didn't open my womb to bring forth. When I lay at night my prayer is always to give God thanks sincerely for you". With my whole heart I give Him praise. "You know", she continue to explain, "the love you have shown me is the agape love much like the love of our Lord; a sacrificial love so unconditional, a love just giving, not expecting. Keep this love, keep this spirit and God will always see you through. It doesn't mean you won't make mistakes or you will not face obstacles, but if you love as the Lord does, He will never leave you". She then kissed the child, the only son she has ever known and walked back to the great house, disappearing as that of an angel.

David glorified God for this wise woman and thought of God's agape love that was shown towards him, not knowing or remembering much of his own mother; all he had was vague memories of her, but God has given him Ma Anna. This mother-figure was one that saw him through the eyes of Christ, not judging or complaining, never expecting, and just always giving. David opened the package and began to indulge of it's contents. The bread and goat cheese with all its fixtures were heavenly. The warm milk was as the sweet taste of honeycomb. Closing the bag, he proceeded to smile for he knew that the remainder of the food was selected with great love and affection. His dad's Range Rover truck emerged from the back of the property and David immediately entered the vehicle.

The journey was a long and lonely ride but was made less lonesome; for in moments as these he focused on his passion, 'worship'. This particular day was no different; he sat back and began to hum a tune as this was usually how the words would form. He thought of the grass, flowers, the singing birds and all of nature, and his song was birthed. "Lord You're worthy oh so worthy, we cry Holy", "all the heavens declare you and earth salute you, Lord you're worthy of our praise". He pulled out the note pad from his tattered back pack and wrote the lyrics down with all the others that were birthed in the spirit. It must have been an hour in travel time but the song remained in his soul. David thought to his self, 'Lord You are so faithful, You reveal yourself in words and deeds even in nature itself. How can we not praise You'? The vehicle came to a stop; they proceeded to exit the vehicle. After gathering all his belongings he entered the facility going through a high tech security scan while being greeted by the welcoming smiles of men, ringing in one tune, "good morning our worshipper". He smiled and declared, "He deserves all our praise". He then made his way to the lower level of the sixteen floor building. There was a slight delay as it was the beginning of the week. Familiar faces poured in, as the work day was already in full gear.

David thought of how unusual his surrounding was. Every person he worked alongside was already an adult and he wondered how different it would be to be in a classroom setting as most young people his age. Nevertheless he shook the thought, and began to focus on the assignment set before him. He turned on the high powered equipment making sure everything was up and running. He then ventured from room to room, cleaning and polishing the equipments for what seemed like hours. His thoughts began to wonder, and being yet a youth, David experimented on all the musical equipments in sight. Everyone was focused on their assigned duties but to his surprise; he went into perfect interlude on the keyboard. He was brought back to conscious nature with profound applauses, of people clapping and voices praising. It was then that he realized that "I must have done it again"; but the song was still in his subconscious. As they gathered around him, he went into melodious worship and began to sing the words of the song that was placed in his heart earlier that morning. With a heart of joy he sang, "Lord you're so worthy oh so worthy, we cry holy", "all the heavens declare You and the earth salute You, Lord You're worthy of all our praise, Lord you are Holy". He closed out the mini concert with a humble bow and a shout of Hallelujah to the Sovereign Lord. He then walked into a record press, rearranging it and began to make space for the new equipment. The shipment was expected to arrive before the close of the work day.

Mike, the floor manager, who was also a father figure and a mentor to David entered the room and broke the silence. "Hey prophet", he greeted. This was how he would usually refer to him. Mike handed him a package announcing, "I brought you a bite to eat". David remembered it was going to be a late evening as he had to unload and setup the new equipment. He also remembered that he had already eaten the remainder of food that Ma Anna had packed for him. As they walked across the room, they open a door that led them to the spacious lunch room. They took their usual seat and began to unwrap the package. Mike had always thought of exactly what it would take to get David perked up. He wasn't surprised to see that he had brought him one of his favorite meals. Golden fried chicken and mashed potato with the most scrumptious corn and fresh cornbread on the side and to top it off, a refreshing bottle of homemade lemonade. The men blessed their food and began to indulge in the tasty home cooked meal that was prepared at Heavenly Delights Restaurant owned by Aunt Harriet and Uncle Duane. Oh how David wished they were truly family. Aunt Harriet looked a bit like that which he remembered of his own mom. Heavenly Delights Restaurant was a very successful chain of restaurants across the New York City tri state area. He and Mike had always made frequent trips on their lunch hour or late days to purchase food. This was how David became familiar with the Johnsons' as they were known. Aunt Harriet who was a very sweet and classy lady would always greet him with a smile and the joyous sound of," Praise the Lord little David, how is life treating you today?". His response was always the same, "Hallelujah, the Lord has been faithful to me. This is the day that the Lord hath made; we will rejoice and be glad in it". She would always smile and declare, "I really wish the rest of the world would think like you beloved; oh what a joyous place this would be". Uncle Duane was a handsome man who had the grace of God on his life; after all, the Lord had blessed him with this beautiful woman. He was a prime example of what is meant by the scripture in Proverbs 18 verses 22: Whoso findeth a wife findeth a good thing, and obtaineth favour of the Lord. They were truly a blessed couple and from their union produced two beautiful children. Their beauty was not reflected only on their outside but resonated from deep within. The eldest was a son, Daniel, who was now twenty years old, and a junior at New York University (NYU). He aspires to attend an Ivy League medical school and become a physician in the future. Daniel was more of a brother than a friend to David. He would always provide him with educational materials and when time permits, he would impart the knowledge and wisdom that he had learnt academically with his friend and brother. David was not a mourner or dull spirited young man; he would always bring joy to anyone who the Lord placed in his path. Daniel always believes that the plan of God was transparent on this young man's life. He would pray at nights that the mighty hand of the most high God would mandate the purpose that he had for him. He prayed that the world would see David for who he was; truly a man with the heart of God who does not look at his circumstance but always Glorifying God for the blessing of life and peace. He was always willing to give a word of prayer to anyone in need; he was no doubt a set apart human being. It was evident that God had a master plan and a powerful call on his life. The couple was blessed with a second child, a daughter who was named, Kylee. She was not just goodly to behold but was also anointed in approximately every area of her life; especially as that of an exhorter and a prayer warrior. Kylee was a freshman at Nyack College majoring in Christian counseling. She loves the Lord to another level and also abode in the realm of the Spirit where most people could only dream of. She had a heart for people and could always be found ministering to those who were in distress that lived in the surrounding areas and communities of the tri state area where her parent's restaurants were located. She was also lovingly known as Pastor Kylee and had also bestowed sisterly love toward David. Unlike others, she knew that David was much closer to his destiny. He was as the sea, still for a moment and after a while will manifest a mighty wave; one so huge that one would know only God could have change his course. Kylee would often copy materials that she received in school and bring them home for her young brother; she would always speak into his life with words of power and anointing. She often reminded him, "Little David, the Lord declares in Jeremiah 29:11: "for I know the thoughts that I think toward you, saith the Lord, thoughts of peace, and not of evil, to give you an expected end". These words would always make his days much easier and sleep much sweeter. These were words that would also allow him to reflect and wonder, 'could the Lord have a plan so exceedingly great for a humble youth as me?' There was no one in his immediate surroundings with the exception of Ma Anna that treated him with any kind of affection. The intimate relationship that he built with God led him to realize that the sovereign Creator kept the grass alive as he walked across them; and the lilies of the field, and the birds that sang so harmonious; He was the one capable of taking him from a life of defeat to victory. He could also take him from a humble state and exalt him high above his circumstances. After all the word declares in Genesis 18:14, 'Is anything too hard for the Lord?'; in remembering this scripture he encouraged himself, trusting and believing the one that he knew who fashioned the world was worthy of all praise. No matter what situation one finds himself, this one thing he should know, 'the Lord will never leave nor forsake us'. The Lord had been with David from he was a child and was with him even to this stage. After much thinking, David came back to the reality of his surroundings.

Mike and David ate in total satisfaction even to the last bite. After freshening up, they exited the lunch room. The remainder of the day went by so fast; the new instruments and equipments were delivered and were fitted perfectly in the available spaces. David waited patiently at the exit of the building for the ride that would take him home; and in this moment he was at total solace with God. The day had become progressively warmer, changing the course of nature; making it much easier to enjoy the presence of the Lord. Upon his arrival home, he emerged to the end of the property which he referred to as 'the backside' and felt at peace with God. He oftentimes wondered what it would feel like to abide in total worship. There was also a longing to worship God in total serenity, knowing that his heart would feel connected to the heart of the Lord. There was a designated area at the backside of his tattered cottage where the wind would always blow in a supernatural manner and all of nature would be seemingly at one in worship. The peace of the Lord could always be found at this place. In this place he would speak to his Heavenly Father, the One who was his refuge and fortress. He understood that for one to be totally committed, one must dwell in the secret place of the most high. He would meditate on verses from Psalm 91: 'He that dwelleth in the secret place of the most high shall abide under the shadow of the Almighty. I will say of the

Lord, he is my refuge and my fortress; my God; in Him will I trust'. David would always find joy and peace of mind in knowing that he had a Savior that gave him unconditional love. As he continued to wait, he removed from his pocket, his 'paper pad' and wrote a song of praise that had ignited in his spirit. As time went by, words of new worship songs were birthed. The presence of God was upon him and it was as if he was in heavenly places, walking in the glory of the Lord. He was visualizing the angels and the elders in worship. He continued to write as the joy of the Lord was his strength. David felt like he could go on for hours. There was a force drawing him to a place; taking him higher and deeper in the things of God. David could vaguely remember his neglected childhood. He had begun to flourish and had drawn closer and closer to the presence of the Almighty God. He was matured beyond his years and favored in more ways than he could imagine. He reflected on the words Kylee spoke with such surety, that the promise of God covered his life. At that moment a feeling came over him like never before; like God had open the portals of heaven over him. The Lord was opening doors that man was never able to close. God had begun the miraculous in his life spiritually.

CHAPTER 2

Summer was now here, which meant that the season would be out of the ordinary for the business. The departure time for David and the driver shifted half an hour earlier. As they walked toward the vehicle, alongside him was a male figure that stood 6 feet 3 inches tall and weighed about 230 pounds who bore strong resemblance to him. They walked from the main entrance of the house and began the journey which was mostly in silence each day, except for occasional questions that would only require a yes' or no' response. David looked at the professionally dressed figure with dark shaded designer glasses that complimented his brief case and time piece on his wrist perfectly. For some strange reason he felt an overwhelming joy and silently praised God for the grace upon his father. Mr. Manner was not a man who was religious or spiritual as some would call it. Nevertheless he was still the one God had chosen to be his earthly parent. He was considered to be very successful in the world's eyes. He was CEO and owner of Manner Equipments. Mr. Manner was a renowned genius nationally and internationally for his taste and unique designs of musical and stage equipments. David however, saw his father as a man of much authority and power that only God could have explained. As far as he could remember, his father was the one who was around to provide his basic needs; but not expected to nurture or be affectionate.

David was the youngest offspring of the Manner children but he never expected to be pampered and often times wondered why his relationship was different from that of his siblings. Many would believe that he would have the best of both worlds; to be employed and also to reside with his father. David begged to differ, as none of the above statements reflected his living condition or his relationship with Mr. Manner. The Lord had given him a peace that passeth all understanding and he understood that his father gave him what he was capable of in this season of his life. Mr. Manner was one who was brought up from a very humble beginning and had worked very hard to accomplish all that he had achieved. He was very sharp both in his professional and personal life. There was not much interaction with him and his surviving relatives. David could only remember seeing one of his father's younger brothers many years ago.

He had lost both his parents but had made them comfortable in their latter years and had relocated them to the warmer region of the country; he gave to them the best money could provide. David's prayer was that God would touch his father and deliver him from the bondage of worldly success. Going through life as a wondering sheep, the reality was, David felt more at peace with his spiritual connection than his worldly possessions. The Lord was the missing factor in his father's life; success had become all that he desired and he ensured that it was accomplished in every area. David could not deny the fact that his heart yearned for the release of this man. Many would question why he cared so much for a person who showed no compassion towards him. 'I have so many unanswered questions' David thought; but it was useless to expect that this man was even capable to express the love of a father, so the questions would remain unanswered in his mind. That situation was considered a closed chapter in David's life.

This particular summer was beautiful or what? There was a different feel in the air and things just felt free. David found that he had more time allotted to write and play the instruments and as a result become a phenomenal musician. He was immensely grateful that the Lord had placed him in this environment. It had become obvious that the purpose on his life was to become a musician and this reality made joy fill his soul. He thought to himself 'this must have been orchestrated by God before the very foundation of the world'. He compared his life to his fathers and recognized that they had something in common, 'a humble beginning'. One would never know what circumstance in a person's life would cause them to express themselves in the way they do; these behaviors would manifest according to the ball life throws at them. He had decided in his mind that when the Lord gave him the opportunity to become a father, he would be the best one ever. He would make sure all his children had the same privileges; they would know that each was a blessing from God. David strongly believed that children did not ask to be born but God had ordained every birth whether one chose to believe it or not. Each person has an ordained purpose in the world; whether or not they are accepted by their parents. The one choice that no one had was to choose their parents. It is an honor when the Lord reveals Himself to you and you enter into a personal relationship, knowing that He is indeed your Father. As the word of the Lord declares, 'We should love the Lord with all our hearts and all our soul and all our mind'. If you are blessed to honor that commandment, you are indeed a set apart individual; one who would understand that you have the capability to love even your enemies, and those who hate you or despitefully use you. When you are graced with this kind of love; there is no room for exceptions.

Upon their arrival, Mr. Manner headed to the sixteenth floor to the executive suite. Once there, he closed the door and proceeded to relax in his plush leather recliner. His heart sunk as his mind stayed focused on the son he'd never embrace, wipe a tear from his eyes, or even ask, 'how was your day'? There was something different on the inside that he could not explain; this new emotion was unfamiliar to him. He removed the glasses from his eyes and wiped the unexpected tears that formed and instantly began to flow. He too had questions he needed to ask and he wondered how could he change what had already gone so very wrong. Was there a way to change a situation that seemed to have taken a course of destruction? Could he ever be forgiven for everything that had gone so terribly wrong? As the thoughts rolled around, he shook his head with the intent of dismissing everything that was running through his mind. What he did not know was that God had a plan for him; to change his past mistakes and forgive him for a decision he had made out of brokenness, pain and despair. He truly wanted to know if he could be forgiven for a few moments of pleasure to an innocent person due to his brokenness. Could he learn to embrace his very seed and not look at him as a mere product of infidelity? Oh how he longed to look past the situation and have a paternal relationship with this humble young man. "I see so much of myself in him", "such a beauty to look at my boyish attitude and body language reflected through this lad. Is there a God who can forgive one as selfish as I?"

David had never given up hope on his father. He would pray daily and in closing ask God to give his father a heart of flesh; to let his father understand that he too had a Father in heaven, who is able to forgive all his sin and shame. There was a knock on his office door and Andrea his assistance came in. "You seem to be very deep in thoughts sir", she exclaimed and continued, "penny for your thoughts". Mr. Manner smiled and said grimly, "nothing new, just getting ready for the road ahead". Andrea remarked, "decisions, decisions"; "yes", he replied, knowing in his heart that the decisions in question were totally contrary to business. Who knows the mind of a man but the man himself?

Sixteen floors below in the basement, David was also reflecting. He knew that the Lord would be the only one to hear and answer the fervent prayer sent up for his father. David was fully aware that the enemy is like a roaring lion seeking who he may devour; he tries to keep people in bondage, remind them of past shame, and pollute their mind. David reminded himself that the Lord could deliver his father in spite of the decisions he had made. The Lord, who is the Alpha and the Omega, has the ability to change any dead situation. He has the power to transform stony hearts into flesh; because He is the all-powerful one who speaks to the wind and calm the storm. "The battle is not mine", he muttered, "it belongs to the Lord". It's been a year since David had moved from the great house and was relocated to a deserted run down cottage at the backside of the property. He had never questioned God for the decisions made abruptly by his father; who had informed him that the cottage would be the best place for him to abide in this season. If only David knew that every time Mr. Manner saw him, he was reminded of the Innocent and Godly young lady who was too afraid to just say "no" to him in his state of vulnerability. This was a mistake, he thought that had guilt tightly wrapped around his neck, never to be removed. Tightening his air passage and choking him at the very sight of his son. David remembered that he was never invited to dine at the family table or even attend family functions; however he was thankful to God that he was kept in perfect peace.

There was an anointing that kept David in a realm above the natural, a place beyond human comprehension. He was called and anointed; a vessel whose path was directed by the Holy Spirit. He never understood why he had to discontinue school, while his brothers were given the privilege to continue. Mr. Manner never had the unction to stand up for his welfare or wellbeing. His brothers were all given opportunities to complete their highest level of education as desired. All his siblings had earned either their masters or PhD's in the areas of choice. As these thoughts swirled around his mind, he thought 'life has a way of coming at you to discourage your walk with God'; but he reflected on Psalm 27:10, "when my father and my mother forsake me, then the Lord will take me up". David said to himself,"the fact that I was now living alone is an open door to build a more solid relationship with God, my Daddy.

This part of the property was not strange to him. As a child, David would frequently come and sit by the lake with Anna. She would always be a source of love and support to him. Those were the precious moments where she had the opportunity to minister to him about the great 'I am'. She would also comfort her little David with songs of praise and encourage him to study the word of God in good times and bad. Ma Anna's words always being the same, "The Lord sitteth high and looketh low", "he is a shelter in the time of storm". He looked forward to every visit to this particular area of the property, not knowing that God had a plan for his latter years. As he grew and matured, even in spirit, the journeys were now more frequent and done by himself. He had also given a name to his designated area; he called it "my secret place". There were so many things that were held in secret. He'd now realize that the fact of not sharing the same mother with his brothers was a deal breaker. He had concluded Mrs. Manner's countenance became displeased at the very sight of him. He had made it his point of duty to make their lives less complicated by staying far away from both his step-mother and his siblings. The reality is, she was the woman of the house and he believes that her preferences were to be respected.

It was now about five years that Mrs. Marcy Manner had become ill. Her illness inflicted sadness and as a result, brought unexpected strain on the family as a whole. She wasn't his natural mother, but she was mother to the brothers he loved and he was just as burdened as the rest of the family. He knew that his brothers loved and depended on their mother. She was an ultimate source of strength for them. Cancer had taken her from being a self-assured woman to a weary and frail stature. It was an ultimate picture of despair which made David's heart yearns for his own mother. His question to the Lord oftentimes was not why she had to leave him, but why she never returned. For some strange reason, it seems that no one had the ability to answer these questions; the journey was still a winding road. He was still deep in thoughts, swimming in a spiritual sea; but after this time of reflection, David felt a new peace and assurance. He believed that the Lord will use your most heartfelt situation to bring you to the place he had ordained for you. Mr. Manner's secretary, Andrea was also concerned for her once energetic boss. He had become less focused and his mind seemed to be in other places quite often. For her, it was weird that her once strongly motivated employer who met all his goals and completed all his assignments with excellence seemed so preoccupied and unfocused. She knew the summer called for hard work and dedication as the office would become extremely busy. There were new accounts assigned and many were already contacting her on items they needed immediately. The one thing she knew was, if he didn't get back to his main focus, things would quickly become messy. She contemplated in her mind the most successful ways and what approach to use to get this once fiery man back to his excellent ways.

David busied himself in the basement doing extra chores to take his mind back to his task ahead. He was scheduled to do some restocking and arranging of materials and equipments. Mike was doing an excellent job and sales had increased; this was one of their best years ever. It seemed ironic that the business was at its peak of production, whether the owner was at his best or not. Most days David had to put in extra hours due to the high demand. These extended days were opportunities that David would happily welcome to bond with his mentor. Mike was always willing to be a father and counsellor for his young friend. On this particular day Mike reminded David of his upcoming birthday; unfortunately birthdays were events in his life he wished he could erase. They were usually spent more quietly with only Ma Anna and himself. It was her yearly tradition to bake him his favorite, plain cake with coconut frosting; and this was all David usually looked forward to. David looked at Mike and said, "not for a few weeks". "Hmm", a few weeks is all we need", Mike responded. The staff had plan a well-deserved surprise party to show their love and appreciation towards this young man.

Ma Anna was waiting for David that evening when he returned home. She startled him as she stood in the shadowed, dimly lit path at the cottage door. As she greeted him with the usual warm smile, she asked "how was your day son". He assured her, all went well, but he was just a tad bit tired. Deep down he knew she had felt something and that was the reason for her presence. He knew that just looking at him; she had concluded that his issue was more than being tired. He was never successful in concealing anything from her, whether spoken or unspoken. His smile was grim and immediately, she knew he had been deep in thoughts yet again. She held out her arms and David released himself embracing her with childlike yearning. 'How great is our God', he thought, 'how great is our Lord, who does all things well?' He flickered back the tears and took a deep breath. "My birthday has rolled around again, eighteen you know" he said and Ma Anna looked at her beloved. With her heart now racing, she knew his thoughts were again geared towards his mother. She cupped his handsome face with her small hands and David looked at her intently. David began to question her, "Is she ever going to show up?", "will I ever meet her?" "Ma Anna I'm just afraid that this is going to be my ongoing desire". She made every effort to hold back the tears. She knew how much it had hurt his mother the day she made the best decision for her son. The promise of returning by his eighteenth birthday was voided and any chance of returning for her son was lost a year ago.

CHAPTER 3

The summer revival was coming up and Mike was very excited. At this time of year the youths in his congregation looked forward to one of the most powerful events. Mike was overjoyed and wanted to inform David of the upcoming meeting. He quickly made his way to find David and in his haste he almost threw David in a frenzy. David chuckled, "someone's in a good mood today" Mike smiled, "I have good reasons to" he replied. "It is that time again for our annual Youth Summer Revival"; "in fact it is exactly one month to date". Friday August eighteenth will be the kick off date of what is anticipated to be three days of power packed anointing. David, I believe you should make every effort to attend. David was speechless and thought to himself that without a doubt he would do everything in his power to be there. “Elder Mike”, he announced “I’m honored and you can count on me to do all I have to make this event”; “you just have to speak to your father and we’ll be all set” he said. With that being said Mike returned to his duty of managing the floor.

David was genuinely loved by those in his surroundings; he had an effervescent sense of joy. They all thought he was exactly what they needed in the lower level to bring in the glory of God daily. This young man was anointed at another level. David was on the list of everyone’s prayer; they all believed that God had a supernatural breakthrough for him. What was puzzling however, was the fact that his dad had him working with the laborers unlike his siblings whose very appearance reflected their dad’s wealth. From the outside looking in, David seemed like an outcast or an orphan. What they didn’t know was that it’s his heavenly Father that he was in full relationship with; this made it much easier for him to cope even with his current dilemma. David had not revealed to anyone how the Lord had appeared to him in a vision. Three times he had spoken to him, reminding him that he was a chosen vessel who He had mandated to set a generation free from the bondage of sin and from music that was inspired by Lucifer. His dreams always felt so real; he would awake in amazement to see that he was in his room and not in direct communication with the Lord.

It was about two years ago when Ma Anna had taken David on a visit to one of her usual places of worship, but this time was different. The power of God came upon David and he was saved by the grace of God. That Sunday David made the decision to be water baptized in the powerful name of Jesus. David was completely assured that by his eighteenth birthday, the Lord would find him a Church home as he was not able to attend Church as he'd love to. The days turned to weeks as the time of the Revival was drawing seemingly near. As a matter of fact it was exactly one week away. His spirit was in full gear and he would declare daily, "I will bless the Lord at all times, and His praise will continually be in my mouth. Oh magnify the Lord with me and let us exalt His name together. I sought the Lord and he heard me and delivered me from all my fears." Truly he knew that the Lord had not forgotten his beloved; his heart-felt desire was to love the Lord for the rest of his life.

Mr. Manner made his way to the extreme end of the two acre property that sat on the outskirts of Long Island. He would take these walks frequently in order to refresh his mind from the hectic spirals thrown at him. The Sunday afternoon was exceptionally peaceful. He began to hum a tune in an effort to completely relax himself. He walked at a steady pace while he admired the elements of nature. He proceeded to the clearing while the narrow spring ran freely through the property; he was stunned. David had made his way previously to his designated spot and was in total worship, the voice as of an angel saturated the atmosphere. Mr. Manner listened to the melodious sound in amazement to his youngest offspring. It hadn't been his first encounter hearing his son in this way, but the moment had brought him to a place of complete re-evaluation. He had utterly no control of the tears that ran immensely from face. He continued to embrace the sound of worship as David, unaware of his guest made every effort to serenade his Redeemer. The words of the song blanketed the heavens as he poured out of his soul. "I bow before your presence and glorify you oh most Holy God, I surrender my all to you withholding nothing, You have given me peace as the river that flows from day to day, hold me close an never let me go, oh master and protector of my soul". This man who was known to many for his strength was surprisingly weak at that moment. His son had turned to a higher force for strength in his time of need. He didn't feel like the man many had perceived him to be; he was at the point of lowliness as his countenance fell surely he thought, "I have lost any hope having any relationship with my son". He reeked of the broken promise he'd made to the lad's mother of making sure that he bonded with her son and promised he would never be neglected. Mr. Manner made his way in the opposite direction and as he neared the guest cottage his heart sank with the pain of hypocrisy. The sound of worship immensely filled the atmosphere both far and near.

The days were narrowing down as there were only a few days left to the New Dimension Youth Conference as it was titled. David began to close out the day by checking if all the equipment's were shut down when he was suddenly disturbed by voices singing "happy birthday". He made his way in the direction of the sound. He was completely thankful for the total effort made to bless him by his colleagues. His eyes opened widely in amazement as they presented him with a beautifully decorated birthday cake and instructed him to make a wish and blow out the candles. Mike proceeded to hand him a large package stating, "happy birthday Prophet, enjoy this gift from everyone who has been blessed by your mere presence"; "just a small token of our love". David thanked his colleagues for the kind and thoughtful gesture. Mike had been more than a friend in more ways than one. He opened the door of the cottage and once inside he began unwrapping the package; his heart was blessed as in the box laid everything he secretly desired. God had truly answered his prayers. The footwear and clothing were suitable for the occasion for which he'd desired them; the blessing came in time for the revival.

The following morning David walked to the front of the property with his luggage. Anna stood at the porch waiting for him. They hugged and then she handed him the package she held in her hand, "your breakfast" she announced. He thanked her and hugged her tightly. "I'll see you next week; have a wonderful time in the Lord my son". The vehicle pulled up to the entrance of the property, David picked up the bag and climbed into the vehicle. He had previously informed his father about the invitation to the revival; it was not the easiest task for him, but he'd done it even though he shook in every area of his body. The most important thing was that his dad had honored his request. "Good morning" they both greeted each other politely and with nothing else to say they went into silent mode. The silence was broken as Mr. Manner spoke in a low tone, "I see you're all set", "yes sir" David agreed, "Mike made all the preparation for the weekend. I'll be back on Monday, thank you for understanding what this event means to me". David was happy when Mike had extended the offer as no one had ever truly given him any kind of official privilege as such. David had shared the information with Ma Anna and had also told her how fearful he was to get the permission from his father. Mr. Manner was indeed a stern man and not one he wanted to look in the face and tell him that he was invited to a Revival that would require him to be away for an entire weekend. Anna assured him that the Lord would go before him because God has a way to speak in our time of need. The talk went as smoothly and she had predicted and the exact response from him was "you have proven to be a responsible young man and additionally I know the passion you have for the things of God. Many of us aren't as blessed as you my son. God has blessed you with a special heart; go and be blessed". David was overwhelmed God had answered his prayer.

The day went by quite quickly and he was in high spirits throughout the entire time. David couldn't wait to get to the Church. Mike entered the equipment room and announced "it's time to go get ready, get ready, get ready, the Lord awaits". They exited the facility in Mike's SUV then proceeded on the short journey to his home. They entered the house, and were greeted by the welcoming voices of Mike's wife and daughters. Mrs. Fraser hugged David and welcomed him again to their humble abode, as she called it. He was also greeted by his three beautiful daughters who referred to him as 'our beloved brother'. "You guys have exactly thirty minutes to get the show on the road" Mrs. Fraser stated. She showed David to his room and said "I hope you'll find all you need as I tried to think of everything you possibly could use". David was sure that he would have all his needs met here and even more. He pulled his bag into the bedroom; he looked around the lavished guest room and his heart melted. The room was entirely amazing and he was totally blown away by the hospitality of his new found family. He flashed the thoughts and began to undress remembering that he had only a limited time there. David took a look at himself in the mirror as tears streamed from his eyes. He got changed quickly and was stunned at the transformation the new garments had given him. The Lord has proven again that he was his Jehovah Jireh. The navy sport coat fitted his body and accented the tone of his complexion. They went splendidly with his khaki slacks and mocha loafers. He made his way back to the family room where he found Mike waiting for him; he handed him a small gift box," from me and the family "he said. David thanked him and hurriedly opens the package. There laid the most beautiful watch he'd laid his eyes on. It had diamonds and leather; David placed it on his wrist and it completed his look to a T. Mrs. Fraser made her way into the room followed by the girls "let get this show on the road" she joked. They all held each other's hand while Mike led them in a prayer of divine protection to and from the Service; he also prayed for every family and individual who would make the journey. They exited the house in the spirit of God knowing that the presence of the Lord was already in his Tabernacle. They pulled in the almost already packed parking lot of the Church. People were pouring in in great numbers; smiling faces greeted each other with hugs and kisses. David looked at the Saints with delight and smile to himself, 'God is truly in this place".

Chapter 4

The Sanctuary was in full flow as the presence of God infiltrated the atmosphere; the anointing was amazing all around. Mrs. Fraser and I took our assigned seats while Mike who was known to the congregation as Elder Fraser was directed by an usher to the pulpit. Once seated, I began to worship the Lord in the beauty of holiness. I was truly grateful to God for this timely blessing. Mike's children were all a part of the youth choir; they were dressed in matching attire both male and female. It had made my heart glad to see Abigail, Hanna and Elizabeth, who was also lovingly called Liz all being a part of the coveted choir. The worship team was already in the climax of worship and everyone in the sanctuary was in total reverence. I began to release my whole being in the anointing as self was already slain for me. The music minister, who introduced himself as Minister Alistair, closed out the praise and worship session and handed over the duration of the service to Evangelist Kylee. It was awesome to see the character of God displayed through these young adults; they willingly allowed the Lord to use them.

The power of God erupted in the room as she greeted the congregation and began to praise the Lord in totality, making reference to the scripture in psalm 150:1 to the end. With uplifted voice she repeated the words under the anointing "Praise the Lord. Praise God in His Sanctuary; Praise Him in the Firmament of His power. Praise Him for His mighty acts; Praise Him according to His excellent greatness. Praise Him with the sound of the trumpet; praise Him with the psaltery and harp". With her voice magnified she continued. "Praise Him with the timbrel and dance; praise Him with stringed instrument and organs. Praise him upon the high sounding symbols". As she proceeded to the final verse Kylee invited the congregation to repeat in one accord "Let everything that has breath praise the Lord; Praise ye the Lord". The power of God was moving with high intensity as she invited Minister Daniel to open with the night's prayer. Daniel began to pray and I was totally in awe as he began to salute the Sovereign King. He lifted his voice and glorified God and took the prayer to a deep place in the spirit. He touched on every area that was facing the world; the family, health, brokenness, homelessness, hopelessness, and global issues. In closing he thanked the Most High God for taking control of the entire service and everyone under the sound of his voice was in total agreement with the prayer. I felt the tug of the Holy Spirit on my heart and I was totally convinced that my change had come.

He handed the mike to Kylee who introduced the youth choir, where first lady, Evangelist Edwards led the solo. The song that was chosen to open the service was "when the saints go up to worship". Sis Edwards was phenomenal in the flow of worship and everything was exactly as I expected and even more. David's thoughts went back to his home and he thought of his family and lifted a prayer in his heart that maybe, just maybe someday they would be in one place, in one voice glorifying God. His heart sank even greater when he remembered Mrs. Manner who was impacted with a terminal illness; he prayed that the Lord would touch her sick body and change the course of her life. The hand of God wasn't short or His ear closed. David knew in his heart that prayer could change the most impossible situation. The song came to an end with Evangelist Edwards holding the final note in perfect soprano. The service was handed back to the moderator who thanked the choir for the powerful worship experience. Kylee continued to give thanks and in total amazement she began to introduce me. "We have a very talented young man in our midst; congregation please help me welcome David Manner to the podium". I stood frozen as she gestured me to quicken my steps. I made my way trying to be as confident as I could. I took my position as she spoke, "saints please give the Lord a shout of praise as this blessed brother lead us in another level of praise". She looked me in the eyes and whispered "let the Lord have His way".

I was handed the mike and my heart took a leap but it was nothing a few deep breaths couldn't fix. I inhaled and exhaled while the congregation encouraged me. I greeted Pastor Edwards, his beautiful wife and family, rostrum occupants, Elder and Sis. Fraser, the youth leaders, and the entire congregation; then l lifted my voice and recited the scripture from psalm 34 verses 1-4. "I will bless the Lord at all times; His praise shall continually be in my mouth. My soul shall make her boast in the Lord: the humble shall hear thereof, and be glad. O magnify the Lord with me, and let us exalt His name together", then I continued in a shy laugh, "I sought the Lord, and He heard me, and delivered me from all my fears", in conclusion he said "please pray my strength". He proceeded in one of the songs that were birthed through the spirit. The power of God moved from one dimension to the next as the words came from his spirit. "Glory of God my great redeemer, full of mercy so full of grace, oh Almighty master forever, glory and honor to His name". The presence of the Lord overtook David as he sang with all that he had. Everyone was now on their feet and some were bowing in the anointing. Words continued to flow from his lips. "Worthy worthy is the Lord almighty, how powerful is your name to you me, God you are worthy of all our praise". David thought to himself, 'I knew that I couldn't stop now as the songs continued to take wings of their own'; 'It was evident that I was drunk in the spirit as was most of the Church'. The fire of God was consuming everything in the atmosphere and it was evident that the Spirit took over in a supernatural way. When I was released and back to the natural, I smoothly came to a halt and was released from the pulpit.

Evangelist Edwards was called to introduce her husband who was the speaker for the evening. She announced "it is time for the word". Pastor Edwards continued in the atmosphere of praise as he took over the service and began to worship the Lord in the realm of the spirit; "saints of God, let the Holy Ghost have His way, the Lord is in His tabernacle like never before so bow down and worship Him". The man of God began to preach the word which was taken from Joel chap 2:28-29 which he titled "The Power of the Holy Ghost". The word came forth with power and clarity and total anointing. He concluded the message and beckoned David back to the pulpit. He said "go ahead son and let the glory fall". He took the mike in obedience and begun to lift The Lord's name in praise. The musicians began to play as he repeated the words of the song. "Let your Spirit have it's way, let your anointing heal and deliver in this place, for where your heart is people, there you are also"; "move in this place, change hearts in this place, break fetters, break chains, have your way". The altar was filled with the youths who swarmed it in every sense of the word. At that moment, I made a covenant with God to stay in His perfect will; wherever He leads me I will follow and forever be His and Him mine. The service was now completely in the hands of God as we rested in His arm surrendering to the spirit.

I woke the next morning still basking in the glory of God, 'the first night of the feast was powerful, and exceeded my expectation', David thought to himself. He made his way to the bathroom that was attached to the guest suite. He turned on the rain shower and allowed the water to massage his exhausted body. He felt like he was in a spa on a tropical island as he stepped from the exquisite tub and wrapped his now relaxed body in the oversized towel provided. He opened the bag that held his belongings and proceeded to dress for breakfast with the hosting family. Mrs. Fraser was smiling as she beheld his presence. "You're up surprisingly early; I thought you'd need a little more rest after allowing the Lord to use you in such a mighty way". She poured him a cup of delicious cocoa, and told him to help himself to the variety fruits and muffins available. He thanked the woman of the house, and accepted her invitation by helping himself to a healthy serving of fresh fruits and blueberry muffin with freshly prepared strawberry jam. David felt completely at home, which allowed him to enjoy this morning's meal in comfort. The remainder of the day was spent in the presence of God as he had totally yielded to his source and strength.

Mike lightly knocked the door of the room that housed his beloved guest. David responded to the knock "it's open"; his friend entered the room with a pleasant smile on his face and greeted David. "I missed you this morning the older man beamed, I had to do an errand for Mother Williams, "you remember her?" he inquired of David. "Yes" David replied; "that's the pleasant usher who directed both you and I to our seats last night". Mike smiled and agreed "yes that's the one and only Mother Williams. I had to swing by the Church and deliver the fresh floral arrangement she'd pre-ordered". "Mother Williams is our Head Usher and she never ceased to amaze us by keeping the Sanctuary looking meticulous. She takes pride in beautifying the house of God. David smiled thinking to himself how the Lord must take pleasure in this sweet woman; after all she's made it her point of duty to keep His house looking excellent. He remembered that the first thing that had caught eyes as he entered the Sanctuary was the prize winning display of ivory, tulips and daisies. Mike reassured his young friend to make himself at home and feel free to help himself to whatever he needed.

Minister Alistair was in his assigned position on the pulpit and the praise team was ready to usher the presence of the Lord in the Tabernacle. I took my seat and lifted my thoughts in prayer to the Sovereign Lord, giving him the honor and praise He deserved for choosing even me and for His grace and mercy He continuously showed toward me. I concluded my prayer and began to worship God in spirit and in truth. This one thing I was confident of was that my promise to God was sealed and signed and to Him alone will I give my whole heart. The song rang out from the pulpit as they continued to usher the presence of God with the words of the song by Pastor Donnie McClurkin "Holy". Tears were now streaming from my eyes as the words of the song took me to a deeper place in the Lord. The anointing engulfed me and in that moment everything became even clearer to me. I remembered the days when I would be in total submission and would journey with the Holy Ghost; the Lord would reveal some of His deepest secrets to my spirit. I continued to worship the Holy One in spirit and truth and in that sacred moment the voice of the Lord began to speak to me in a still soft voice, "I have chosen you even in this hour to serve me with your whole heart; I will use your voice to declare to the word that I alone am God. You will sing of my goodness and my grace to encourage the fatherless, the widows, to this generation and even to the righteous, that I am yours and you're mine. Even before the foundation of the world I have called you and your name shall be great for my glory. I AM THE LORD".

The praise team closed out their session and the choir took their position. Mike's children were all seated together and I thought to myself how fulfilling it must've been to be a part of this awesome choir and sing to the glory of God. I was comforted in my soul as the Holy Spirt released me and I felt confidence arouse in me. God was totally in control and His will must be done. I was confident that this was the soil where my soul was planted. Once again the choir was a blessing to me as a solo was sang by a young lady, Sister Destiny. This sister in my opinion was definitely sold out. She led the song "Hallelujah Angus De" with the confidence as that of an Angel. My heart was overjoyed and the presence of God was all over His house. They continued and blessed us by ministering two more of my Favorite songs, one of which was by Tejan Edwards. The choir took their seats as the service was handed over to the night's moderator, a beautiful young Sister Evangelist Ashley James. I thought to myself hmmm, 'could she be of any relation to Sister Destiny James?' oh well, I shook the thought, maybe or maybe not. Mrs. Fraser interrupted his final thoughts as she gently handed him a folded paper. I took my seat and proceeded to read the note which stated that Apostle Edward was requesting my presence in his office. I informed Mrs. Fraser of the contents of the letter and excused myself from the pew and followed Mother Williams as she directed me to my destination. She took me to the second floor office and assured me before departing "go ahead son they're expecting you"; "don't look so surprised, I'm confident that your best days are ahead and maybe even starting now".

I softly knocked the door and it was opened immediately. I stepped in the beautiful room which was freshly scented with leather and pine. Sis Kylee stood smiling along with Pastor and Evangelist Edwards. She greeted me with a holy kiss and told me to take a seat while both the Pastor and First Lady extended their greetings to me. My heart was now racing as I sat across from the man of God and tried my best to compose myself. "Son" he spoke up "I guess you're eager to know why you were ushered here but before we go any further let us pray". We all held each other's hands as Pastor Edwards began to earnestly pray. "Father in the name of Jesus here is thine beloved son. You know all about him mighty God and we thank You for allowing him in our midst. God we place this discussion in thine hand, cover him Lord and continue to anoint Thine beloved in every area of his life, let the will of God be done in his life and have thine perfect way in Jesus name, amen". David he continued, "you know we were extremely blessed with your ministering last night; you are amazingly gifted". "Sis Kylee is currently the National Youth President and is a discerner of spiritual gifts and talents, and honestly speaking I trust her judgment. I know you came highly recommended and we just want you to know that you have a place here and the choice is all yours". "Young man" he continued to speak, "you came highly recommended but besides that, I can clearly see that you're a man of humility who just wants to please the Lord. We were blessed beyond boundaries and the congregation would be honored to have the spirit use you tonight". I was in total amazement; God had answered my prayers. He honors His word and I was now walking in prophetic fulfillment as I was more than ready to give my all on any given night. I spoke up and thanked them for the invitation to minister and also informed Pastor Edwards that the decision is already made on my part. I have found the missing piece from my life, and I'm convincedthat this is where I belonged. Kylee hugged and encouraged me with her usual words "He knows the thoughts He has toward you, thoughts of good and not evil for an expected end" then she began to worship. Evangelist Edwards hugged me with enthusiasm and spoke with excitement, "let me be the first to welcome you to our congregation". Those word rang in my spirit, "welcome".

I made my way back to the congregation, and was met by Mike in the foyer. I informed him of all that had occurred. His response was "be blessed in the Lord my son"; then he turned his attention to the hills. I was surprised to hear him whispering a prayer, giving God thanks for the next phase of my life. The service was now in full flow and the power of God was moving as young Elder Onajhe Morgan was in the midst of his exaltation. He was the first of our two speakers and this minister was doing a phenomenal job as an exegesis. I stood and began to agree with the man of God as he exhorted on the text in 1Timothy 4:12 which was one of my favorite scriptures. He was the perfect example of what was meant by the spoken, “let no man despise thy youth”. The congregation was preaching with the preacher and my soul was encouraged. I knew now that I could do what was expected of me in the excellence of God. The young speaker closed out the word and the next voice was that of Evangelist Ashley, “saints of God”, she spoke lifting her voice with power, “God is in this tabernacle, there are so many young people who are bound to pornography, bound to drugs, bound in depression, just completely lost but here we are surrendering our lives to the work of the ministry. We will not give up on our brothers and sisters”; “come on confuse the enemy”, “worship for your neighbor, worship for your community, worship for your school, parents worship for your children, grandparents worship for your grandchildren, uncles and aunts warship the Lord; as Bishop Jakes who proclaims it best says, with lifted hands of praise we pronounce war on satan and his kingdom, yes PUSH(pray until something happens), yes can you hear it?; chains are broken and the devil is defeated. Our young people are being loosed; give God a shout of praise and cry, FREEDOM”. She was now in the depth of the Spirit and speaking in tongues as the Spirit gave her utterance. Sis Kylee walked to the podium and held the woman of God as they worshipped the Lord God. The moderator called my name and introduced me again to the Church. I made my way to the pulpit and once there, the same anointing that was over me was magnified. I greeted the Church and the relevant officers in their respective offices. “Saints” I remarked, “truly I was blessed on last night and I’m just in awe at the present moment that the power of God has moved mightily thus far. My determination is to please God and Him only; the Lord has given me the privilege to be before His people I don’t take for granted the mantle that’s been placed on my life. I want to thank the Lord for Apostle Edwards and our first lady and the presidential staff of this youth department who has entrusted me to minister to you”. I signaled to the musicians and began to let the Holy Ghost have His way in me. The anointing moved upon me and I was taken to a dimension beyond human comprehension; it was all in God’s hand now.

David lifted his voice and worshipped the mighty God. “Let us exalt the majesty on high; His name is Jesus, the one who bled and died for us all. He has risen, His name is great, and greatly to be praised”. “I know some of you might even be tired but I pray you’ll be in agreement with me; for when I think of the goodness of Jesus and what he’s done for me, my soul cries out hallelujah, thank God for saving me”. “The Lord is looking for a remnant who will love Him with all your heart, all your soul, and all your mind”. The young people were hungry for the anointing and I went directly into the ministry of songs. The atmosphere was charged as I began to sing from one song to the next as I was led by the spirit who was navigating me. The glory was now thick in the house as many were bowing before the throne of grace while others were in total submission. As I closed out the session, the Lord unctioned me to release the message to his people; "thus sayeth the Lord", "my people I will release you from fear and bondage, from brokenness and pain, for I am your GOD, I am full of mercy and compassion, for I am GOD". "Thus sayeth the Lord". I went back to my seat worshipping the name of the Lord. Mrs. Fraser held me in a holy embrace and begun to pray my strength, asking God to give me vitality and rejuvenation. The final speaker, Minister Daniel approached the podium in the same anointing and opened the Bible. "Saints", he announced, "please turn your bibles with me to the gospel of Saint John the fourth chapter and verses number 24". He continued "My Lord has done a shift, lets praise Him for the ministry of our young bother, the appointed and anointed David Manner, my brother from another mother". The people began to lift their voices in oneness, thanking God for me. The preacher continued and went straight into the scripture as was declared. He stated "I will use a topic tonight, bow down and worship Him". He went into the spoken word moving in the fullness of God. I was totally blown away at how he brought the word with fire; it was palatable. The Lord was indeed feeding His sheep; what more could we ask the Lord for? I thought; He had abundantly blessed us.

The next morning I woke up totally rested and realized that I was revived in every area. "David", Mike ringed my name with enthusiasm, "come and join us". It was Sunday and the last day of the feast and I anticipated it would continue in excellence as the previous days. I walked to the man of God in the dining room where the whole family was gathered to dine before we got dressed for Church. I made my way to the front of the open concept living and dining space. This house was as beautiful as one that had stepped straight out of a magazine. The hardwood floor ran entirely through every room; the kitchen was classy with matching countertop and an island made of waterfall granite in ivory and silver. The back splash was a sight to behold in beautiful emerald and gold; the farm sink was grand, the cherry finished cupboard with silver handles was in total alignment with the stainless steel appliances. This house wasn't just beautiful; it was also a Sanctuary that was reeking with the peace of God without and within. I joined the family at the dining table being totally grateful. I sat down and recollected how I was never invited to dine at the table of my own family. Mrs. Fraser had totally outdone herself with this setup for the meal. I thought this was meant to be a mini banquet; the table was beautifully set and sitting in the midst was the best looking homemade pancake, waffles and array of fresh muffins along with the fluffy scrambled eggs that looked delectable, topped off with turkey bacon and sausage. Mike sat at the head of the table and lifted his voice as he blessed the meal that was obviously prepared with love, and then announced "let's eat". We ate our fill all engaged in conversation on what had occurred in the previous services and was eager to see what the Lord had in store for the last day of the feast. We ate our fill with the exception of the cook, who exclaimed that she was full just preparing the food.

"David" Abigail spoke up, she was the youngest of the three; a sassy outspoken young lady who said exactly what she perceived in the spirit. I looked at her with earnest expectation and wondered what was up Abbey's sleeve. I hesitated then answered nonchalantly in my softest tone, "yes ma'am"; everyone at the table chuckled, as it was discerned by them that I was aware of her outspokenness. David didn't shy away from her; he opened his heart to receive her this time. "I just want to say how God has truly used you in this conference", she raved "oh my word, did you see how many souls were saved and many have even received baptism by water; when the Lord gets ready you have to move and no devil can delay or deny". "Wow" she continued, "I've heard dad speak of the relationship you have with the Lord but I must admit, I was amazed at the move of God on your life while in worship". I looked at her intently and smiled in appreciation but no speech was uttered from my lips. Mike who was usually silent in these moments began to agree with his youngest and began to participate in the conversation. "David" he spoke with authority, the sound that was more of a father than a friend. "Yes sir" I replied as he continued to speak; "son you know there's no turning back now" he reassured me. "The scripture declares in Matthew 6:6, as the Lord urges us that when you pray, go away by yourself, shut the door behind you, and pray to your Father in private. Then your Father, who sees everything, will reward you publicly". Mike had seen the passion this young man possessed towards his Savior and on many occasions would make an altar in the storage room where he often shuts himself away in submission and consecration to the Lord. He had been a blessing not just to one but as many as the Lord had brought in his path. Mike said in closing "My son, truly your change has come". Mrs. Fraser and the children shook their heads in agreement and all resounded a strong "amen". I was not smiling anymore as I knew every word that was spoken had already been revealed to me. We wrapped up our breakfast session as Mike and I volunteered to clean up, allowing the women to get a head start.

I cleared the table which was covered with the most exquisite and regal dinnerware set I'd ever laid eyes on, being as cautious as I knew how. Immediately after, Mike loaded the dishwasher and stared the load. We then retreated to our rooms as we too had to be on our way. It was the final day of the feast and I knew the Lord was saving the best for last. We had at least an hour before our scheduled departure. I entered my space and reached for my Bible and as I held it in my hand, tears instantly flooded my eyes. In that moment I suddenly reflected on the one who had given me this treasure. My Bible was a gift from Ma Anna on my twelfth birthday and it was my most prized possession;

after all it was the uncompromised word of God that giveth life. I held the leather bonded book in my hands and began to make supplication to the Lord. I knew that I was to be the psalmist for this morning's service and I needed a word from the Lord. "Dear Lord" my words came from a sincere heart, "open up the eyes of my understanding today as I seek you in more ways than one, oh Lord hear my humble cry". I then opened the Bible and breathed silently then said "speak Lord, thine servant heareth".The pages opened to me and I looked at the word in total amazement. The word of the Lord that ignited in my Spirit was Jeremiah 1:5, which reads "before I formed thee in the belly I knew thee, and before thou camest fort out of the womb I sanctified thee, and ordained thee a prophet unto the nations". My heart was overwhelmed with joy knowing that the Lord had sought me even in my lowest state.

The car came to the entrance of the building; we entered the parking lot and exited the vehicle. I walked briskly to the Sanctuary as there was an unusual spirit of boldness upon me. I was acknowledged by the greeters who welcomed me with a joyous heart; I then made my way to the altar. I opened my spirit to receive from the Lord waiting to hear what He had orchestrated for me. I was released from the altar and began to make my way to my usual seat, when I was stopped my Mother Williams who spoke "son, your seat today is in your respective place". I looked at the beautifully well attired lady and was just taken aback by her flawless appearance; she was dressed from head to toe in white apparel which made her look more like an Angel. I thanked her and followed her lead and was met by Kylee who greeted me with a holy kiss. I greeted the Ministers, hugging Daniel and young Minister Onajhe Morgan, who was the eldest brother to Evangelist Ashley and Sis Destiny. They were all Grandchildren of the splendid Mother Williams. The choir was taking their position on the pulpit and Minister Alistair led the praise team; the sound of worship brought everyone to their feet. The service had officially began and I was now totally relaxed as this was truly home. The choir sang and I was in awe as the power of God emanated on young Sister Destiny as she led the choir in worship. The moderator was in high spirit and sang like a bird as the choir closed the last note "we are a chosen generation, call for to show His excellence, all I require for life God has given me, and I know who I am"; "I know who God says I am, what he says I'm, where he says I'm at, I know who I am". Each young person under the sound of the ministering of the choir was now on their feet, worshipping the Lord exclusively.

The next hour went by with all protocol in excellence; Apostle Edwards who was called to the pulpit declared "the final day of the feast is in fullness of the glory of God", "it's raining" he elaborated; "the harvest is ready, come get wheat, come get barley, seek and you will find". I extended my hands to the heavens and my heart to the source, for only He could've supplied all my needs in the way that it was overflowing with grace and favor. I began to meditate and rebuke the lie that was often told by the deceiver, who frequently whispered words of deceit leading us to believe that our drought will last forever. We oftentimes think that we're forgotten, but God who has redeemed us from the curse will never leave or forsake His chosen. The great I AM has promised to even leave the ninety nine and go after the one; "my sheep" sayeth God "knows my voice and another they will not follow". Pastor was beckoning for those who were empty to come; he said "don't wait until the service is over, the altar is open for whosoever". There was an abnormal passion in this wise man of God I thought; his heart was for winning souls. Each person that was prayed for made their way back to their seat.

Evangelist Kylee made her way to the podium and her voice was now trembling in brokenness; she tried her best to compose herself in order to get the next phase of the service in the manner that was expected. "Praise the Lord beloved" she greeted the Church, "the word of the Lord in the middle of the holy Bible, Psalm 118:24 declares "this is the day that the Lord hath made, we will rejoice and be glad in it". "I dare somebody to give the Lord your best praise and watch God move the mountains blocking your blessing". "My job here is a fairly easy task"; "I was commissioned at this moment to stand here and introduce to the blessed and highly favored family of God, a young man who has made the Lord the center of his life". "Saints of God, coming to us one more time is our young psalmist, David Manner"; "he has revealed to me that he truly lives according to Psalm 37:4 which reads", "delight yourself also in the LORD and he shall give you the desires of your heart"; "this young man has a passion for true worship". She shouted "let the Lord have His way as we get to the next level of glory". I stood at the podium and she held my hands and squeezed it to let me know that it was well. I took my position and extended my arms to the heavens and declared "Saints, all glory and honor, dominion and power is to be given to the most High God, who inhabits the praises of His people". "I declare war on the kingdom of darkness in this season"; "let us worship the Lord in the beauty of holiness". The power of God began to fill me in every area as I proceeded to magnify the Lord and began to sing with my whole heart. The notes were perfected on my tongue and I realized that nothing was being done in my own strength. I opened my eyes and standing before me was a sea of young people, many who had never moved in any of the two previous services. I closed out with the words from the song "My Will", by the incomparable Tejan Edwards. I was saturated in the spirit and in the natural as I released myself and handed the mike to the moderator who was also under the immense power of the Holy Ghost.

Bishop Wayne Brown made his way to the pulpit; he was the vessel chosen to close out the last leg of the revival. This man of God journeyed all the way from London, England to deliver a timely and effective word. The power of God escalated to a higher level as the man of God began to lay his hand upon me, releasing a double portion of blessings. "Son" he announced, "the word of the Lord over you is yea and amen". "Thus sayeth the Lord-you were chosen even before the very foundation, to proclaim my name in season and out of season""; "to every nation on the face of this earth, be blessed and go forth in Jesus name". I held my hands up in complete surrender and glorified the Lord for this declaration. The preacher opened the word and instructed the congregation to stand before the Lord and open their Bible to the mandated scripture, Romans 8:1; the people stood in reverence as the man of God began speak in the authority of God. He instructed each person saying "grab your neighbors hand and look them in the eye and tell them that my prayer tonight is that the Holy Spirit will move in them"; "now look your other neighbor in the eye and tell them the same word, amen". "Now this one is personal-put your hand on your heart and declare, Holy Spirit move in me". "I don't have to go over the preliminaries that I'd intended because our young minister David, and don't get me wrong the choir and the praise team did a phenomenal job this morning but God mandated this man of God to bring in the presence". "Now the word presence means pre-sence, we had the presence of the Holy Spirit"; "someone felt the pre-sence that the Lord is in His house". "Saints of God" he continued, "we will read from Romans

8:1 and then we'll skip to verse 9, 10 and 11; thank you Jesus hallelujah". "Brothers and sisters I don't know who's in this house tonight"; "you weren't going to come but you braved the elements and you're here tonight". "God is releasing a divine shift for you and by the end of this service you will receive a supernatural miracle from God". "I'm going to read Genesis chapter 1, you don't have to go there; I'll just read and you follow". He read the word with pre-eminence and then it began to take root in me. I began to see the scripture in a total different light. He closed out in verse 5 and lifted his voice, "I speak this word even now", "there is a line that the darkness cannot cross". "I declare to you once again that by the end of the service there will be a separation of light and darkness in this place". "We are the children of light and we'll let our light shine and win this city"; "in order for us to win a city, Lord move in us".

The power of God moved once again as the young people began to worship their God and magnified His name. As the praises began to subside, he began to read from the chosen text Romans 8:1. "There is therefore now no condemnation to them which are in Chris Jesus, who walk not after the flesh, but after the spirit"; "turn to your neighbor and say-neighbor you're not condemned". Verse 9 of the text reads, "but you are not in the flesh, but in the spirit, if so be then the spirit of God dwell in you; now if any man have not the spirit of God, he's none of His". "You need to know my brothers and sisters that in fact the spirit of God dwells in you!"; "but anyone who doesn't have the spirit of God is none of His". "Now lift your hands to heaven one more time and speak to yourself with authority and say-God move in me!" The word was now rooted as the Saints lifted their voices in one accord and repeated the words. The Bishop lifted his eyes to Heaven and directed his prayer to the Lord declaring, "Lord use us to win this City, change what the enemy meant for bad and turn it around for good, in Jesus mighty name". "The blood of Jesus is saturating this environment even now". "The blood invokes change, causes blessings, deliverance, and transformation"; "the blood will allow healing to take place due to its presence in this house". "Lord we thank you for the Angels that are in this house, guarding this place and carrying blessings throughout this Sanctuary". "Lord bless every individual with a heart for souls". "I pray this prayer in the mighty and powerful name of the Lord Jesus Christ, amen". "I want to speak to the body of Christ because we're excellent doing church that some of us could be referred to as churchian"; "but God did not call us for such, His call is for us to be Christ like". "Saints coming to church doesn't make you a Christian; this is not the time to play church, we need to desire an intimate relationship with God". "Worship Him at all times"; "yes I agree that we all have struggles, but that's an indication that you are called of God". "The negativity in your life is a result of the call". He looked intently in my direction and continued to speak again. "Children of God" he spoke with surety, "the most precious stone known to men are diamonds, but in order to retrieve this precious stone you have to dig deep in the dirt as they're buried deep in the earth compressing them together for many years". "When most diamonds are discovered, they come out as black as coal, but inside that crucible of suffering there is a stone of great value"." Many of you are as such-a diamond in the rough"; "give God a shout of praise that today you are coming out".

The man of God was moved by the spirit and began to prophecy in accuracy over the lives of the Saints from one extreme to the next. I had now recognized that the Lord was on an assignment to loose His people from bondage. The enemy had no option but to get out of the mind, the body, the will, and even the way of God's children. My mind reflected once again on my father and brothers and I began to seek the Lord earnestly for their hearts. I knew I was chosen without a doubt; I also knew the Lord is not a respecter of persons. The scripture in St. John 1:12 specifically declares, "But as many as received Him, to them gave Him power to become the sons of God, even to them that believed on His name". I exhaled and gave the Lord thanks in advance for the victory over my family. The Bishop had now made his way to the altar where both the saved and unsaved were being delivered by the blood of Jesus. It was amazing to see God move in such a miraculous way. The sick were healed, the oppressed also stood believing, and the bound were loosed.

Apostle Edwards, Elder Michael Fraser and the ministers believed God for miracles at the altar. The service was now in the overflow. I smiled at my friend Elder Michael Fraser and whispered to him "thank you"; "today I've experienced a life changing move of God, one that would stay with me forever".

Chapter 5

I woke up to the sound of birds tweeting as a melodious orchestra; although we were in the city the sweet sound of nature resonated in the atmosphere. The sun was now beaming on my face as to say 'good morning'. I exhaled and glorified the Lord for one more day in the land of the living and surrendered my heart and soul in honor of the one who is my maker. I made my way from the plush comfort of my bed which was now customary for the few days I had been in this domain. With my mind and thoughts directed to the Father, I offered up my prayers before Him believing that it would go up as a sweet smelling savor. The words came from the depths of my soul as I prayed in total supplication. "Lord you are my LORD, thou art high and lifted up and there is none like you, from everlasting to everlasting there is none that is like unto you. You created all things for your glory and for your glory only. Thou art Alpha and Omega, the beginning and the end; oh Lord I will exalt your name forever, to you I offer up all my praise. Lord as I humbly bow before you, purge me with hyssop and I shall be clean, wash me, and I shall be whiter than snow. Create in me a clean heart God, and renew a right spirit within me. Behold I was shaped in iniquity and in sin did my mother conceive me. Thank you Lord for life and life abundantly. God I put this man of God and his household before you, thine beloved Elder Mike Fraser, an anointed and appointed vessel with the love of God buried deep in his heart; oh God touch his mind and continue to open the portals before him. Bless Missionary Fraser and their beautiful children. Anoint this family individually and collectively from the top of their heads even unto the souls of their very feet; thank you Lord for giving me such a family as this man of God". My heart was in total submission as the earnest need to continue to pray was birthed deep within me. It was as a burning fire shut up in my bones; I adhered to the call and went as I was led. "Lord" my voice now softened "let God arise and the enemy be scattered, cover the woman of God my beautiful spiritual mother Ma Anna and comfort her soul in my absence, give unto her the joy of thine salvation and bless her evermore. Lord touch my Pastor Apostle and Evangelist Edwards and their beautiful children Anna Christina, Joshua and even their unborn child; oh Lord thank you for the Johnson's who are nothing short of divine blessings, my dear Uncle Duane, Aunt Harriet and their blessed children Minister Daniel and Evangelist Kylee. God continue to anoint them in every area of their life. Lord touch my church family, meet their needs Lord whether it be spiritual or natural, bless the body of Christ on a whole and anoint them afresh as your word declares in Ephesian 6:18 'Praying always with all prayer and supplication in the spirit, and watching thereunto with all perseverance and supplication for all saints'. Thank you Lord for being Savior over all, bless the man of God Bishop Brown and his family, cover his wife and children, bind every weapon that comes against this family in the powerful name of Jesus". I allowed the Lord to navigate my every thought and lead me to higher heights and deeper depths.

This was now my secluded moment to serenade my God and King, the lover of my soul. In total surrender I glorified God with my whole heart, giving Him all the glory that was due unto Him as my mind reflected on the scripture in the book of Revelation chapter 4:10-11 which declares 'the four and twenty Elders fall down before him that sat on the throne, and worship him that liveth forever and ever, and cast their crown before the throne, saying, thou art worthy Lord, to receive glory and honor and power. For thou has created all things, for thy pleasure they are and were created'. I thanked the Lord for endowing Judah in me; even if you are in Lodi bar the Lord will lift you up just to become one in him. I must have been lost in worship for close to two hours and I realized that time goes by quickly when you're basking in His presence. The time was far spent and it was time well spent in divine prayer and worship. It was 9:15am but the time was not of relevance as Eder Mike had managed to get us a leave of absence; I smirked and entertained the thought, 'a leave well deserved'. I thank God for His favors toward me and I made myself comfortable as I continued to send praises to the Most High God. I opened my bible and turned to one of my favorite scripture St. John chapter 1 and began to read the word of God as my very life depended on it because the word of God was what had kept me and I saw it as life and hope; I truly don't know where I would've been had it not been for the Lord on my side. There was a new man in me, one who had a change of mind and I was ready to submit my all to the Lord. The revival had birthed my destiny and I was ready to go where the will of God would take me. I closed out my time of consecration and thanked the Lord for giving me this time so I could completely retreat to His presence. I lifted my body from my prostrate position and began to make the king sized bed with the luxurious bedding, totally ignoring the instruction given to me be by the lady of the house, that it was her pleasure to dress the bed in her desired way. With the completion of my duties I took a step back and admired the job that I had done and chuckled to myself 'hmmm not half bad even for me'. Matter of fact it looked as beautiful as the first day that I'd walked into the room and wondered to myself 'wow, fit for a king'. I opened the door that lead me to the ensuite bathroom and began to undress from my sleepwear making my way to the spa. I turned on the rain shower head to the massage option and allowed the water to revive my aching muscles; I didn't really mind as they had occurred from a time well spent in the presence of the Lord on the previous day.

The aroma from the kitchen was enticing. I made my way to the front of the house and saw Elder Mike sitting at the dining table with his bible opened and seemed to be in deep study. I tried my best not to distract him but he closed the word and motioned for me to take a seat. "Aw" he said "I thought you'd surface, did you rest well? I heard you in worship and prayer"." Amen" I said agreeing to all the above. I sat across from him as he poured me a cup of herbal blend tea and as he began to pour the sweetener he asked me if would I like a bite to eat; I accepted his offer and he made his way to the oversized refrigerator and began to prepare sandwiches of different assortments. We blessed the meal and began to indulge in my choice of cold cut, cheese, fresh tomatoes and leafy green lettuce with my choice of dressing. I ate my fill and was totally satisfied with the choice of meal. Mrs. Fraser joined us in the kitchen making her way to the unfinished meal she was preparing, "how are you mother" I inquired "oh I'm blessed" she beamed "truly blessed, what a time we had in the Lord". "Yes ma'am" I agreed, "sorry it had to come to an end" I joked, "amen" they agreed. "I pray you have a huge appetite for dinner today son" Sis Fraser spoke up "I'm preparing your favorite; curried goat served with fluffy pigeon peas and rice, creamy potato salad, sweet and tangy coleslaw, and fresh avocado"; "hmmmm" I thought, but it didn't stop there, she informed me that she was also going to prepare a refreshing cold sorrel beverage just the way I loved it; sweetened to taste with lime and ginger. "Yes I do" I replied and blessed the Lord quietly for His love towards me; this meal was totally invented with me in mind. I thought of Ma Anna who always knew what it would take to put a smile on my face; a serving of tender curried goat would always bring sunshine on a cloudy day. "We'll be dining in fine style today" Elder Mike added, "all to your honor; we are so grateful that you've blessed both the revival and our home with your presence, you are truly a blessing David Manner, a true blessing from the Lord. We need you to feel welcomed among us knowing that our doors will always be opened to you; you are family and we don't take for granted that the Lord allowed you to cross path us". My heart was full of joy and I was exceedingly grateful; my tears were more than my words as I hugged the man and woman of God and assured them that I was very thankful for the hospitality they had all shown towards me.

Dinner was everything I'd anticipated and more. The meat was exactly the perfect texture and flavor; everything was exactly the way I liked it. Mrs. Fraser really out did herself and I truly appreciated the kind motive. We ate and all wore a look of satisfaction as the family engaged in the topic of the youth revival, 'win the city'; everyone was charged and ignited to go into all the world, and preach the gospel. We were convinced that Apostle Edwards had truly heard from the Lord in this season. The times were becoming extremely wicked and the enemy was as a roaring lion seeking whom he could devour. We all agreed that we were on the war path to win the Kingdom for the Lord. We all had our fill and I began to make my way to the bathroom when the phone rang. Elder Mike answered the call and greeted the caller "Praise the Lord" which was the custom of the household. "David" he called my name with urgency "this is your call". I made my way in his direction as he handed me the device with joy. I greeted the caller in like manner and waited for the response. "Praise the Lord beloved one" the caller greeted back; my heart was now going at a little faster pace when I recognized that it was the voice of Pastor Edwards. "Hi David, I hope I'm not calling you at an inconvenient time"; "no sir" I replied "it as good a time as any, we just finished dinner and I was about to head back to my room, but I'm not in any hurry" I assured him. "Great" he beamed, "ok then I'll just go directly into the reason for my call. I have a proposal for you and I think it would be more fitting if we could meet face to face; I can be there in ten minutes, would that be ok with you?" I looked at Elder Mike and he smiled mischievously and nodded in approval. Apostle Edwards was at the door in the exact time he'd promised. The man of the house opened the door for the more than welcomed guest; we all greeted Pastor with enthusiasm then I was instructed by Elder Mike to make my way to the study. We took our seats and Pastor led us into a prayer that would allow the Lord to have His divine way. "Son" he continued after closing out the prayer "this task is not an easy one before me but I'll go in the grace of God". "Son" he continued, "do you mind me calling you that?" "Absolutely not" I responded politely. "Amen" he smiled "well I'll just get directly to reason of what brought me here on such short notice. I was informed by some reliable source and by that I'm making reference to our own Elder Fraser, the Johnson's, with solid recommendation from Sis Kylee who truly believed she had complete conformation by the Holy Spirit through much prayer and fasting and accurate discernment. The church has been in a time of intersession seeking the face of God for an anointed young minister to assist Minister Alistair in the office of music ministry and during the course of the weekend the Lord has proven to us that He's heard our humble cry. David I know you are exactly what the body of Christ needs in this season, and according to Elder Mike you've made the decision to become a permanent member. I know this might not be an easy decision for you to make, but I hope you'll pray about it and let the Lord lead you". "Son" he continued "there is an open door, in which the Lord has set before you that no man can close in Jesus name". I listened intently and allowed the man of God to get his point across, knowing that only God had made the impossible possible.

Apostle Edwards looked intently at me with uncertainty. I knew he was for a moment at a cross road; at least for a moment. I smiled in his direction to release an assurance and immediately his posture straightened to a place of confidence; his countenance was restored to his usual pleasant state. I knew the opportune time was at hand and recognized that the word I'd spoken had come to fruition; God had stepped in and released me in a supernatural way. I had made a decision as far as I could remember to get closer to the Lord as soon as my eighteenth birthday rolled around. I had served my father and remained humble to his beliefs; I hadn't exasperated Him in anyway concerning my passion to serve in ministry. This call had been my lifelong desire and I'd waited patiently on the Lord. I knew that this was one of the major concerns in my mother's state of brokenness, when she had to make one of the most important decisions of her life. She had released me in my father's care with binding document that stated he would be the sole guardian until I was at the age of legal consent. I released my thoughts and began to thoroughly examine my surroundings and the opportunity that was set before me. I thanked God sincerely for the doors He continually opened before me; truly this was the appointed year of release and manifold blessing, which lead me to what Ma Anna had often spoken in my hearing. "In the appointed season the Lord will open doors no man can close, and likewise close the doors that men will not be able to open". Apostle Edwards broke the silence and spoke in a mild tone "remember now David you are not being pressured, take as much time as you need as there is no rush in getting back to me". I looked directly at the man of God in front of me and spoke in a spirit of gratitude, "that will not be necessary; I have already made the decision to become a member of the family of God and that the Lord would have His way in every situation". "Sir" I continued "my answer to the proposal is yea and amen". The men of God both breathed a sigh of relief. I chucked and uttered the statement to both men" truly you must have known that this was ordained of God; when Jesus says yes nobody can say no". We all laughed in unison and Apostle Edwards extended his hand and shook mine stating, "well I guess this is as good of time as any to welcome the newest member of our ministry". I thanked him and hugged Elder Mike who was now beaming from ear to ear.

I walked back to the family room where the women were all gathered waiting with a look of anticipation. I looked at the beautiful family who stood before me and asked in sarcasm "are you guys ready to have me as your permanent weekend guest?" The women shouted ecstatically and began to embrace me with tear filled eyes, while Abbey spoke in a trembling voice "Lord you truly gave us the desires of our hearts, welcome home my brother in the Lord". Mrs. Fraser smiled at me and said "your place is here for as long as you need; you're just the same to me as one of my own". I made my way to the bathroom and then to my room kneeing before the Lord with thanksgiving in my heart for all He had done for me; I then made my way back to the family room. Mrs. Fraser had told us earlier that dessert would be served and it was promised to give total satisfaction. We all gathered around the coffee table while the woman of the house brought the mystery dessert on a silver platter; she was totally right in her promise as the smell of homemade sweet potato pudding filled the atmosphere. The splendor of fresh strawberry and sliced peaches was topped with savory whip cream and if that wasn't enough she topped it all off with the all-time favorite, grapenut ice cream. We had our fill as we engaged in a discussing of the path that I'd chosen to take and ended the night in prayer and thanksgiving to the Lord.

As we made our way to work the following morning, I was still in a state of amazement of all that had occurred during the course of the last few days and I made a vow to Jesus that this was where I always wanted to be; in the secret place of the most high. This was definitely a life changing experience and I was at the point of no return, believing and walking by faith. So much has been birthed in me within the days spent in the youth conference and in the time spent in my room in total submission. Elder Mike interrupted my reminiscing with a prayer of thanksgiving unto the Lord for His mercies that brought us safe thus far. The day went by quickly as I was focused in getting my duties done in excellence unto the Lord and not man. It was about midday when I heard an unusual footstep getting closer to the stock room.I straightened my posture and made my way to the entrance of the room and was startled by the surprise visit of the owner and CEO of Manner's Production, none other than the man himself, Jessie Manner. I stood frozen in a distant gaze wondering to myself what I owed to this totally surprised visit. I was sure he could hear every beat of my heart from a distance. He looked at me in total dismay and smiled in an effort to break the ice and began to encourage me "don't look so surprised" he greeted, but that was an understatement; It wasn't a surprise, it was more of a shock. He dismissed my silence and continued to speak in a normal tone." I just came by to say hi and to let you know that Anna misses you terribly" then he continued, "so how've you been?" I mustered up all the courage I had and answered him with total sincerity of heart "I'm doing exceedingly well; truly the Lord has been good to me". He smiled and said "well it's great to have you back, see you soon". I lifted my voice to a steady tone and replied "yes sir". He left the room and headed back to his exquisite office space. I walked to the main showroom and sat at the closest seat available and made myself as comfortable as possible. I was totally disappointed at the way this meeting had gone; 'wow' I thought to myself, this didn't exactly go the way I'd always dreamt it would've gone. Anyhow, I knew that the Potter was doing a new thing in my life and as declared by Ma Anna 'if there is an open door, then my Lord wouldn't leave any stones unturned'. This was my father and I loved him in every sense of the word; I realized that the Holy Spirit was doing a work in him and I am fully aware that the Lord can make even the impossible possible. God is truly a way maker and a problem solver. I rose from my brief rest and continued to finish my final task, anticipating the time of my dismissal.

Elder Mike sat in his office on the main level of the building. I knocked the door and as a sign of respect completely ignoring the fact that he'd made it clear to me on many occasions that all the formality wasn't of relevance. He looked up from the pile of papers and spoke "knew it had to be you, but I won't waste another one of life's precious breath to convince you to just enter my office unannounced". "To what do I owe the pleasure of this visit" he questioned with a mischievous tone. "The pleasure is all mine" I teased. I asked for his permission to close the door for a brief moment, he looked at me and quickly assured me to go right ahead. Mike rose from his desk and walked over to the young man in front of him who was obviously in a state of release. "You ok son" he inquired, "yes" I replied "never been better, truly the Lord is great and greatly to be praised". I told him all that had previously transpired and how the Lord was already making a way for me to walk in my inheritance. He looked with joy and agreed to my professed words; "David" he continued "what God has done, no one can undo so walk in the promise". I left his office and made my way to the stockroom retrieving my personal belongings and headed to the parking lot to the spot that read 'reserved for Jessie Manner'. I stood beside the white year to date Range Rover and began to wait in patience for my dad. I waited for a short while when I heard the sound of the familiar alarm and the unlocking of doors which was my queue to enter the vehicle. I sat in the passenger seat anticipating his arrival and going over the proposal I had.

The car door opened and Mr. Manner entered the vehicle, placed the key in the ignition, and looked in my direction saying "would you like a piece of gum", I thanked him and extended my hand and accepted his offer. We started the journey home and I began to prepare my mind for the next level of conversation. We were a few minutes into the commute and the traffic was flowing steadily; there was a peace in my spirit knowing that the Lord had already made clearance. I took a napkin from the holder in the glove compartment of the car, removing the gum from my mouth and proceeded with my proposal. "You ok?" he broke the silence "yes sir" I instantly replied, and cleared my throat; he smiled and shook his head. I took another moment then spoke in a confident tone, "sir I was waiting for the right opportunity to inform you of the proposal that was given to me this past weekend"," ok" he replied. I began to explain all that had transpired to the best of my ability, from the greatest to the least detail and everything in between; he listened intently allowing me to express all that was of importance. I closed out my last sentence and told him that in order for me to accept the proposal I would like to be closer to the ministry. He looked at me with deep sincerity and gratitude and the words began to freely pour out of his soul, "David" my father spoke my name in a deep tone "you have my blessing, I know that this is exactly what your mother would want for your life. She gave you this name and trusted you in the care of the Lord and I know that your best days are ahead of you; thank you for allowing me to share this milestone with you". I thanked the Lord for showing up and allowing me to see a part of this man that was never revealed to me before.

I got up the next day to my normal routine thanking the Lord for His mercies that are new every morning; I made my way to the shower and entered the throne room to glorify the God of host. My heart was yearning and my soul thirsted for my one true love. I allowed the Lord to saturate my spirit and began to give unto my Savior what was due to Him. I lifted my voice and began to worship the Lord in the beauty of holiness. I made my way to the Great House and began to reflect on the mighty move of God that had transpired in the conference. I was thankful to the Lord for the great opportunity that He had prepared for me being an assistant to the talented and anointed man of God in the person of Minister Alistair. God had placed me directly where I needed to be in this season of my life.

The morning was as beautiful as one could ever imagine; the sun was shining beautifully and the air was sweet as the scent of fresh lilies. I was on the final stretch of my journey when my eye connected with the small stature of the woman that anticipated my arrival. Ma Anna was waiting and a broad smiled adorned her face as she made her way to meet me with enthusiasm. With her arms outstretched the tiny figure held her beloved and tears began to stream down her narrow cheeks. Her thin lips were quivering as she wipe the tears revealing her beautiful hazel eyes, "I missed you greatly but the Lord gave me rest and peace knowing that He had you in His shelter. How are you? Your countenance is glowing I know you are revived; did you receive what you were anticipating in this meeting?" Ma Anna took a deep breath and began to apologize "how will you answer these questions if I never allow you to get a word across". David giggled and touched the mighty woman of God on her shoulder as they made their way to the patio.

David took the closest seat to the exit of the house and spoke in a low tone full of affection and respect to the woman who had always showed motherly love toward him. "I missed you the few days we were apart; you were always in my thoughts because the memory of you always brought me joy. I want you to know that you have a very special place in my heart and I will forever be grateful for everything you have done for me". Anna smiled in acceptance of his gratefulness and for keeping her promise to his mom. David never took for granted how she would have a warm meal along with a note that consisted of vital bible scriptures on the small table in his cottage; it was always a meal that was both satisfying to his body and also his mind. He began to muster the courage to tell her all that occurred on his trip and prayed she would also give him her blessing. The conversation went even better than he expected as he told her of all that had transpired in the conference, inclusive of every important detail, expounding on how the Lord had blessed him in every step of the way. He excitedly informed her lastly of the call that was placed on him as an assistant minister of music. Anna listened with joy and congratulated her son with a shout of hallelujah to the Lord. "My child" she began to speak with authority "God is just beginning; the Lord is getting ready to take you beyond boundaries and I know you are ready to receive from the Lord so turn up your cup because the anointing is getting ready to flow at another level. I'm thankful to the Lord for allowing me the privilege to see His work while I'm still in the land of the living. I know that you were chosen and if there was ever a time for the Lord to do a mighty work, it's now. Our young and old alike need to see the move of God through the younger generation and it's not purely speech, it just facts. God has placed you in His perfect will and groomed you in His excellence, and is ready to use you as His mouth piece to declare to a people that He's still on the throne and He rules on high and reigns forever". I looked at the woman of

God in amazement as she ministered to me and confirmed all that was spoken to me by the Lord; I had no other choice but to glorify the Lord for His favor toward me.

The week went by quickly and Friday was finally here. Ma Anna was waiting for me by the patio and greeted me with her usual "good morning how was your sleep?" I smiled and answered in my usual manner "my sleep was sweet". Anna looked me in the eyes and reminded me saying "oh yes the good Lord watches over his beloved"; "well I guess this is the day of truth" she continued, "I pray the Holy Spirit will guide and protect you as you venture into higher heights and deeper depths; my heart is with you, go fort to that Sanctuary and let humility be your portion. Remember to keep the agape love ignited in your soul always". She then took a few steps toward the door of the patio and reached behind a huge patio chair and proceeded to hand me a black mini travel case that was also doubled as a back pack; "go ahead beloved this is for you. The good Lord dropped it in my heart to get you a few things I thought you will need". I looked at her in a state of amazement and spoke in a whimper "for me?"; "yes for you, I told you the Lord instructed me to move and do as He had spoken concerning you. Now go ahead and open it; what are you waiting for, Christmas"? I took hold of the beautiful genuine leather bag and realized that this was not an inexpensive piece of luggage. I began to open the bag and my eyes bulged; I was in a state of shock as the contents were revealed. The bag was neatly packed with care. I gently examined the first piece of clothing which was a navy blue Polo Ralph Lauren cotton pajama and matching bed slippers, lily white tube necked t-shirt, three of the most beautiful basketball shorts my eyes were ever privileged to behold, a package of white ankle socks, a grooming set which also consisted of a brush and comb, and lastly, a deep brown leather journal. "Ma" the words came out with great joy "you shouldn't have", "oh shush child, it was always my desire to do this and more but I didn't want to seem intrusive with the likes of your father and all; anyway the Lord has given me clearance and boldness". I began to arrange and repack the luggage when she spoke again in urgency "you aren't finished". I looked again as her face lighted up as the morning sun, "go ahead she declared open the secret compartment". I began to look in the first pocket but she ended my search and directed me to the secret pocket that was covered by a flap which made it very impossible to locate. I proceeded and opened the compartment effortlessly as it was left unlocked. My heart took a fast beat or two as I remove the package which revealed a white case with a cell phone but not just a cell phone it was an IPhone, yes an IPhone six plus; I was now at the point of speechlessness and definitely convinced that she had totally outdone herself. I opened the case removing the phone and walked over to the motherly figure standing with joy in her eyes; the tears were now doing their duty as I hugged her small frame and thanked her repeatedly. She held my hand and squeezed it firmly and uttered the word I knew was coming "I love you baby". The truck drove up to the entrance and I hugged her for the last time and proceeded to the vehicle with my prestige overnight bag and the warm package that consisted of a fresh sausage, egg and cheese croissant, a golden banana and a bottle of cranberry juice.

I entered the compound in great spirits. Elder Mike was waiting for me as I made my way to the basement. "How are you?" he asked politely, "I am blessed and highly favored, truly the Lord is great and greatly to be praised", he smiled at me and replied in agreement "yes He is, indeed He is". We both chucked and continued to the lower level, "are you all cleared and ready to go to the next level?" he spoke with a sense of importance; "as ready as one could ever be" I replied. "I can see that" he teased and began to scrutinize my luggage. I laughed and joked back "it took you long enough" I said "yes, Ma Anna got me exclusively ready for my weekenders". I was in high spirits through the course of the day as my heart was filled with joy as I worshipped God with my whole heart; I did my duties with the joy of the Lord, who is my strength. The work day came to a close and I made my way to the first floor and knocked on Mike's office door and informed him that I would meet him in the parking lot. I walked to the elevator and continued to the sixteenth floor; the door opened and standing before me was my father. He greeted me with a welcoming smile. "I was just making my way to see you before you go" he said, "seems like we are both in the same mind frame". He didn't give me a chance to respond as he extended his hand placing an envelope in mine, which had my name on the front; just a little something I thought you could use. I accepted the package and thanked him then stated in a low voice "I'll see you on Monday", "on Monday I will" he replied. I pressed the button of the elevator and proceeded to make my way to the main lobby, when I heard my name. "David" my dad called out "have a great weekend", "thank you" I said and waved as the elevator door closed. My mentor and friend was awaiting me in the parking lot with a look of concern on his face. I told him what had transpired and he breathed a sigh of relief. We arrived at the house in great timing and Mrs. Fraser met me at the entrance and hugged me with delight which made me realize that truly our feelings were mutual. I greeted her and entered the house where the girls were all gathered in the family room harmonizing. I stuck my head in the room and began to greet them when Liz called my name and spoke in a sweet gentle voice, "not so fast we've been waiting for you". "You have a question?" I asked, "yes" replied Abigail and Hanna. Elder Mike interrupted our little chat and chastised his daughter's saying "can you let the young man at least put away his belonging?" they all answered together "yes daddy". I entered my bedroom which was pleasingly scented with the indulging scent of spring and was totally impressed by the personalization's that were applied. The oversized dresser was beautifully decorated with three hand crafted picture frames that housed photographs of me captured at the youth conference. I quickly place my luggage in the walk-in closet and made my way back to the living room.

Mrs. Fraser was in the kitchen at her usual spot and I stooped in first and thanked her for the new look and also all the new additives; she smiled at me saying "it was a team effort, glad you like it". The girls were beaming from ear to ear and I knew that I was truly home. We sat around the fireplace as they convinced me to join in one my favorite songs 'Invitation ', by Byron Cage. We sang in total harmony filling the house with praise; we were interrupted by Elder Mike who called us to the dining table. We took our seats as he said grace and began to indulge in golden brown country flavored homemade fried chicken, tasty barbecue ribs, golden corn on the cob, creamy mashed potatoes, homemade dinner rolls and of course Mrs. Fraser's signature Caesar salad. We finished what to my description was a meal prepared with absolute love. The time had been far spent so I returned to my room, got into the shower and prepared myself for the youth meeting.

Kylee met us at the entrance and greeted us as she teased "well it's high time you royalties got here". We greeted and proceeded to the sanctuary when she interrupted me and spoke "not so fast mister you follow me". I was about to inquire about the change of direction when she informed me that I was needed in the office. She knocked the office door and Pastor Edwards answered "it's open", "go ahead" she said "he's expecting you". I entered the office and was totally surprised to see that he was not alone. Bishop Brown sat with a youthful smile on his face as I took the seat which was gestured for me to take as the greeted me. "This is David Manner" he said officially introducing us, "a young man with a powerful future; God has anointed him in this season to reach those who were otherwise unreachable, those that had been discouraged with the religion and are seeking a relationship with their maker. I know that the Lord has brought him from a mighty long way and I am determined to stand behind him every step of the way". Bishop Brown extended his hand and shook mine with power as he stated, "it is a pleasure to meet your acquaintance son, I was abundantly blessed through your ministry and I realized that you are in total submission to the Holy Ghost; that's all the Lord is looking for, not ministry but those who will completely surrender to the His leading". "David" Bishop Brown continued "be not afraid or dismayed but be strong and very courageous; remember the race is not for the swift but to those who can endure to the end". I looked at the Bishop in total agreement and began to reflect on my purpose. I thought to myself 'the Lord had really favored me; it was I that had been distinctively blessed beyond comprehension by this appointed vessel'. Bishop Brown was a man after the very order of God yet he spoke with such humility. Apostle Edwards broke the silence by explaining the mandated reason for the brief meeting. "Bishop Brown was sent here on assignment today to lay holy hands upon you and anoint you with oil". I nodded in agreement and bowed, surrendering to the Lord. The man of God proceeded to anoint my head with oil, then laid his right hand upon my head and began to pray in the spirit. The glory of the Lord was thick in the room as we all began to glorify our God in the spirit as well as the natural. I was immediately taken into the third Heavens and beheld the glory of the only begotten of the Father and my soul was now at rest. Apostle Edwards closed out with the final prayer as Bishop Brown went on to say to me "keep your eyes on the one above and remember, hell is on watch because the enemy knows of the call on your life; the devil is literally trembling even as we speak, knowing that the Lord has chosen you to break barriers and invade his camp through your purpose. Don't give him any room and keep this scripture near and dear to your heart, 1 Thessalonian 5:22 which declares, Abstain from all appearance of evil".

CHAPTER 6

I sat on my favorite smooth rock enjoying the scenery in the cool of the day on the backside of the two acre property of my father's house. It had been three months since the conference and my life had gone to another level of commitment. My focus was now to sincerely render my all to the service of the Lord. I lifted my eyes to the hill from whence my help came, meditating on the one who was the author and finisher of my life. So much had occurred in the last three months. I came into contact with so many different personalities both saved and unsaved; many who were utterly disappointed at life and some who had just simply lost hope and were willing to give up on life entirely. My heart was broken for those who felt that God had distanced Himself from them. My commitment was to win a generation for the kingdom by any means necessary with the help of God. My perception according to the word was that the Lord was not a respecter of persons and what He has done for one He will do for another. Ma Anna oftentimes confesses that God is always the same and He never changes; He's the same God yesterday, today and forevermore. I closed my eyes and allowed my thoughts to be swept away by the Holy Spirit as I listened intently to the sound of nature. The birds were singing in sweet melody and the sound of the wind in the trees made the combination of a melodious orchestra in total harmony. I was now in the midst of Heaven's chorale; I was in the spiritual realm totally in the presence of God. In this place of worship, I was supported by the trunk of an apple tree as I laid my head in the cushion of His arms. I was completely immersed in the anointing and I began to inquire of the Lord 'where does He want me to go from here'. I knew that it was because of His grace and favor why I had even made it this far. I wanted to be the one who would serve His people with total sincerity of heart; at that moment my mind became one with the Lord.

The thing I remembered in the conscious moment was reflecting on the scripture James 1:5 which states, "If any man lack wisdom, let him ask of God, that giveth to all men liberally, and upbraided not; and it shall be given him". I was transformed and found myself standing in the presence of the Lord in the midst of the garden and the scenery was beyond anything I could ever imagine; this garden was divinely planted and nurtured by the Lord himself. The garden consisted of flowers of all different colors, shapes and sizes; the splendor of the grass was in uttermost brilliance. I began to admire my surroundings in amazement as the journey seemed like there was no end to the beauty that was set before me. I began to sing songs of praise to Jesus my Lord and with every word that was released from my lips, a light shone more beautifully on the garden. I was inspired to worship the Lord in a dimension, each time being taken higher than before. The glory of the Lord was now upon me and everything in my surroundings; I began to bow in reverence before the Lord and even the grass and flower was now in total obedience to the Most High One. I continued to lift my voice and the words that were transported from my soul was filled with the wisdom of God beyond what my natural mind could comprehend. At that moment I realized that I was being taken to higher heights and deeper depths and my mind was totally transformed. I closed my eyes in an effort to subdue all that was before me and it was then that I heard a voice echoing my name. I immediately opened my eyes and standing before me was the biggest wings I'd ever seen; I began to cover my face and continued to bow but the voice was escalated and spoke with authority saying "arise and don't be fearful". "I was sent by the Lord, I'm only a messenger"; "David the Lord has heard your fervent prayer and your request has been granted"; "the Lord has filled you with His wisdom and now you will go and do as you're instructed of your God". "Remember the word of the Lord declares that whatever you desire when you pray, believe you receive it and you will have it". I was now directly face to face with the one who was speaking to me and I opened my mouth to speak but there was no one there. I began to walk to the end of the garden and out of the wind came the voice of power and authority. "David", I heard my name another time and began to look around but beheld no one. The voice continued to speak "look at the flowers I've set before you and behold their beauty, for they shall be to you as a representation of the people that I've set before you. Look for the inner beauty in everyone and see their future as bright as that which is arrayed in this garden. These flowers were not always as beautiful; some needed more attention than others but with tender loving care they have all blossomed to their full potential and are able to give glory to Jesus Christ to whom all honor is due". The words had become life to me and I listened with my whole heart as He instructed me. "David it is now time for you to go, but let not this word depart from you because you are chosen as the one who will show the love of God to all who has a desire to know him; just give what you got and let the Lord do the rest. My son you have a task before you now, so go and release the agape love, for I am your God and I'll never leave or forsake you".

The day had receded, and I was finally released from my vision. My heart was set completely in the will of the

Father. The days were becoming progressively colder and fall was in full effect; the trees had lost all their leaves but that was only a sign that we will go through transitions in different seasons of our lives. I was working alongside Minister Alistair and was humbled to be under his tutorage. He had served as the sole music minister for the past two years. He was at least ten years my senior, happily married and had a beautiful baby girl who was now three years old. Alistair was an insurance agent by profession and I wasn't sure if that was the reason for his stern mannerism. I had not been completely successful in building a bond with him and this had made me very troubled in my spirit especially due to the lack of communication between us. I walked into the Sanctuary with the hope of changing the course of our relationship. I made my way toward him and was very optimistic that today would be a change and maybe I would get his focus; I was hoping we would get off to a better start. He sat at the piano and I was impressed at his expertise so I applauded him as he concluded the final note. I greeted him with a smile and extended my hand toward him but was crushed when he didn't return the gesture but uttered "how are you?" He began to make his way out of the room but stopped abruptly and stated in an apprehensive tone "you know the annual Christmas Gospel Explosion is two months away and Evangelist Kylee has requested that you work with the younger group that ranged from ages fourteen to twenty two. You are required to be here every Friday and

Saturday for the next couple of weeks. I apologize for the short notice as this was totally neglect on my part; however I'm convinced that you're more than qualified to get it done" he spoke sarcastically and left the room.

David's stomach began to feel as if there were a thousand butterflies dancing around in it, but he quickly reminded himself that he could do all things through Christ which strengthens him. The youth service had now begun and as he was previously informed, he was chosen to lead the praise and worship session along with the worship team. David went before the Lord in transparency, inviting the presence of the Almighty God. His heart was totally stayed on the Lord the entire time as they sang unto the Lord and he reminisced on his previous vision, knowing that he was in the perfect will of the Lord and he was committed to stay steadfast. He closed out the session by singing "total praise" by Richard Smallwood. Sis Elizabeth was the night's moderator and she was spiritually charge and ready for the next level that the Holy Spirit had promised 'prepare us to win the city'. We had an awesome time in the Lord and were now in the last leg of the service when Sister Destiny graced the pulpit with the announcements. She reminded the church of the Annual Christmas Gospel Explosion and the voices were magnified as everyone began to glorify the Lord for the long awaited event. She did her best to maintain the attention of the congregation and spoke in an exited voice "Saints, last but not least in the announcement, our own Brother David will be overseeing the youth choir with those of us between the ages of fourteen to twenty two". She had hardly gotten the update out when there was an uproar of praise and she realized that the Lord had truly favored this young man. She waited for the atmosphere to come back to normalcy and closed out by declaring "are you ready to step into another level?", "are you ready for higher heights and deeper depths?", "are you ready to encounter another level of worship?", "say amen if you're ready" and everyone agreed in unison. "Our first rehearsal will commence tomorrow at 6:30pm sharp, followed by 6:00pm on Fridays starting next week". "We will be taking advantage of every opportunity we have and trust that the Lord will do the rest". Immediately following the announcements, Pastor Edwards closed the service and everyone made their way to congratulate David.

The weeks leading up to the events were electrifying; we would meet for practice and go into a time of prayer and intersession allowing the Lord to have His way in everything. I knew in order for us to be true worshippers we had to first die to self and self-will. The Holy Spirit led us to the scripture in Saint John chapter 4:23-24 which declares 'but the hour cometh, and now is, when the true worshippers will worship the Father in spirit and in truth: for the Father seeketh such to worship Him. God is a Spirit and they that worship Him must worship Him in spirit and in truth'. This moment of meditation allowed us to reflect on the goodness of the Lord and His mercy towards us, for one must acknowledge that it is He that chooses us. I was grateful for this opportunity and knew I would not do anything in my strength but only God's will be done through me. I thought to myself that I had the most cooperative and willing young people on this side of glory. Our rehearsals were going even greater than I expected and the hand of the Lord was on each person individually and collectively. The sopranos, the tenors, and the altos were all on one accord as they worshiped; the sound was a harmonious rhapsody that left you in a glorious state of mind. Destiny was chosen to be our lead soloist as she had a perfect combination of melody and could divert from a soprano to an alto, magnifying to the uttermost or receding, allowing the flow to move in excellence. The song that was chosen for us to minister was "Indescribable" by Kierra Sheared. I was totally blessed at the selection as every word of this song exalted the name of Jesus and allowed me to be my true self giving Him all honor and glory.

We were ready for the Gospel Fest and everyone had put in more than we originally planned. The team went above and beyond what was expected and Destiny made my job less demanding; the young lady had the voice of an angel that was destined to change the atmosphere wherever she went. We were at the close of one of our last rehearsals on Saturday, giving God praise for His blessings toward us when my thoughts were interrupted by the cheery voice of Kylee as she hugged and greeted me. "Praise the Lord my brother from another mother". I hugged and greeted her with enthusiasm "praise the Lord sister of mine". She continued "well I see you guys have made it through in one piece, are you ready for the big night?" she questioned; I paused momentarily then chuckled "ready my dear beloved" I spoke in a voice of correction. "Ready would be an understatement, this choir is definitely headed for greatness and Sis Destiny is truly superb in every sense of the word". She smiled and at me in an inquisitive way and continued "David I have some additional news for you; we received an update from the Gospel Fest committee and they're requesting for each church to minister a solo selection. I pray you would do the honor of representing us this year"." I know it is short notice but I'm convinced that you will definitely get the job done". This came as a surprise but I knew that I couldn't say no to this woman of God who believed in me against all odds. I looked at her straightway and assured her that it would me my pleasure to represent this ministry.

I returned to work after my weekend, and waited for my Father in the parking lot as it was my routine at the close of day. Mr. Manner entered the vehicle and we started the journey home. We started out in the normal silence and gradually began to break the silence with "how are you, how was your weekend?" I was excited and began to speak out of the norm, updated him of all that we had accomplished as a choir. He listened intently with a smile and I knew that he was pleased to see how happy I had become in these past few months; he knew that outside of my job and the church, all I had was Ma Anna. He was relieved to see how open I'd become and the guilt had lessened for him because he saw that I was not alone. I looked at him and knew that he was deep in thought but I knew I had to share the events of the Gospel fest with him. "Dad this is going to be a very powerful event as we will be among some of the best choirs and among the greatest in the gospel arena"; "I was also asked to minister as a soloist for that night". He drove slowly as he pulled into the driveway and turned off the engine. He looked at me with joy in his eyes and with urgency in his voice said "David that's awesome and I will make every effort to be there". "I know that this will not make up for lost time" he apologized, "but I will try my best to support you in every and any way I can". "I know I've not been your greatest supporter in the past but I hope you'll give me the opportunity to make amends". His words touched my heart and I realized that my prayers were being answered in a timely manner and I shook my head in agreement to his promise. He began to exit the vehicle when these words came fluently from my heart "dad I just want you to know that I might never completely understand the choices that were made concerning my upbringing, but I want you to be clear on the fact that I will not hold a grudge towards you or my mother. Everything the Lord has allowed me to experience on this brief journey of my life has only been a process that has strengthened me in ways that I wouldn't otherwise experience if He wasn't my only source. God was a Father and at times a mother who was always there in my time of need". "Please dad" I continued to speak in an earnest tone, "you left me in the most capable hands-the loving care of my Lord and Savior Jesus Christ". My father sat quietly and smiled as I poured out my heart; my word released him from years of guilt and torment. We left on a good note that night and as I made my way to the cottage I began to thank the Lord for all His promises towards me; only God could have done such a work on this man. The God of the impossible is capable of changing even those situations that seemed stagnant or complex. He is a heart fixer and a mind regulator; one touch from our Savior can remove every dead thing for He came that we might have abundant life. The cottage door was unlocked and I entered my room with a feeling of relief that evening. I quickly made my way over to my twin sized bed and bowed in reverence before the Lord. The words came from the depths of my soul as I began to intercede for my father, my mother, and all those who'd made choices that had held them in bondage.

It was a couple of days before the Gospel fest so I went to Elder Mike's home on Tuesday evening after work, with the blessing from my father. We were required to rehearse every day until the Friday before the show. We drove up to the church building and Mike went to his usual spot in the parking lot. I made my way towards the sanctuary and noticed that the man of God was right behind me, "you don't mind me sitting in on this session do you?", "I really just wanted to see my son in action", "the girls are very excited for where you have led them in such a short time". We were now in line with each other in our strides and I looked at him and told him that it would be a great pleasure for him to be my guest. We greeted the choir and Minister Alistair and went directly in prayer and meditation as was customary. The session went by without any glitches and the worship was explosive; there was no doubt in my mind that the Lord had been with us every step of the way. Sister Destiny was at the peak of musical perfection and it gave my heart joy thinking to myself that surely this flight was ready for takeoff or as the older folks would say 'this ship is ready to sail'. Elder Michael closed us out with a special prayer of blessing and guidance for the final days ahead.

"David" I heard my name from a distance and looked around to see Minister Alistair beckoning me to approach him; as I made my way back to him, my mind was at rest knowing that the Lord was in control. "How are you?' he greeted, "I see you've made every day count and I just wanted to commend you on the fact that the choir is doing exceptionally well. "Thank you", I politely answered him but realized he wasn't finished speaking. "Remember that I will redeem my choir after the Gospel fest and I wouldn't want you to be too disappointed as I don't give up easily on what belongs to me"; "just thought I should give you a heads up". I was astonished at the words that he spoke with such authority but the Lord anointed me with boldness and the fear that was once there had left me unaware. "Brother Alistair" I looked him directly in his eyes as I spoke, "might I remind you that all things belongs to the Lord for his glory and His honor only". "I am very aware of your position in this ministry and I give honor where honor is due, but let me inform you that I'm not here on my own accord", "let it be known to you this day that I'm only about my Heavenly Fathers business". "I know you have not been the friendliest person I've met in my brief time here, but I want to remind you that the Lord will lead me with or without your support, for what the Lord has ordained he will maintain". The conversation was interrupted as Mike called me from the exit doorway of the Sanctuary. I held out my hand and this time I made sure to take his in mine and shook it with love, "have a blessed night my brother" I said with a heart of sincerity and made my way to the parking lot. We met for the final few days and surely the power of God was in our midst at all times. Minister Alistair was even more withdrawn than usual but I knew that he had allowed the enemy to lie to him and he had allowed the spirit of jealousy to creep into his soul. I was determined however, not to be distracted by the enemy and his schemes. The meeting was only two days away and we were also in the final days of our fast, hence the devil was mad; I also knew that he was defeated and God was already victorious.

My alarm went off and I looked over at the clock on my bedside table, it was now 3:00am Saturday morning. My clock was set to alarm every three hours until 3:00pm. I made my way to the floor and bowed in reverence before the Lord and began to seek His direction in everything that He would have us to do. I recognized that the grace of God was on us and was truly blessed by some of the testimonies from the young people. I had done all that the spirit had instructed of me in my vision. The word of the Lord unto me was to imagine people as flowers and they will flourish with love and care. I was determined to stay in the presence of the Lord in intersession, prayer, and consecration until the closing of the fast. The clock made its final alarm and I made my way for the floor one final time and stretched before my Maker in a prostrate position as I glorified Him with all that was within me. I rose to my feet with the revelation that He was the potter and we were the clay and each of our destinies was in His hand so I left my room with a feeling of joy.

Mrs. Fraser had prepared lunch and we all sat at the table and indulged in the tasty roasted chicken, roasted potatoes and fresh vegetables. Abigail was very delighted as we ate and would eagerly remind us that time was at hand. It was a beautiful day as we arrived at the venue, Madison Square Gardens in New York City. We gathered our belongings from the coach and I looked around my surroundings and realized that this has now become a reality and I was ready for the next move of God. I was immersed in His glory and the anointing was visible all over me. I wasn't the same person who had entered the Sanctuary a few months prior at the youth conference; surely the Lord had wrought a work on me. The Auditorium was lavish and grand; we were led to our designated area where the capable staff of pleasant men and women awaited us. We were instructed on all that was expected of us from the entry to the exit of the stage, from the greatest to the least detail. We went our separate ways to our dressing room; I was deeply impressed at how we were treated and as I sat in the room I began to reflect on my life and recognized that humble beginnings does not dictate your life. There was a light knock on the door and my thoughts were interrupted, "who it?' I asked; the voice on the opposite side of the door replied "Pastor Edwards". I opened the door and was met by a surprise visitor; standing before me wasn't just my pastor but I was graced with the presence of Bishop Brown. He greeted me with the biggest smile and teased "you didn't think I would miss this event did you?"; "I flew in from the UK to see the debut of the incomparable David Manner". They were both standing in the middle of my room when Apostle Edwards asked my permission for them to pray one more time and anoint my head with oil. I immediately fell to my knees as a sign of submission to the Lord as the men of God lifted their voices and covered me in prayer of protection; they completed the prayer and left the room assuring me that it is well. I stayed before the Lord in the selfsame position and glorified Him in the beauty of holiness, being convinced that the power of God was never to be underestimated. I had never revealed to anyone of what had occurred between me and Minister Alistair but our God was omnipotent and all knowing, and because He is my banner He had sent his agents to cover me in this critical time.

The program was now in progress and we met one final time as a group to pray before our performance. We then made our way to the left of the stage where we were able to see the performances. The band was playing as the praise and worship team opened the pre-show. After a few minutes, the lead worshipper closed out and the MC welcomed the next item. My eyes almost popped out of my head when none other than one of gospels greatest, Donnie McClurkin graced the stage. He opened the night with a prayer of thanksgiving to God and glorified Him for affording us one more year to be in this setting as we came to glorify the Lord and lift up praises to His name. I was drawn even closer in the spirit through the anointing of this man of God. The choirs began to make their way to the stage one after another and ministered in the spirit of excellence that was blessing my soul. The program was released to a half hour intermission; we headed back to the dressing room where we had light refreshments while discussing the nights happenings thus far. The intermission came to an end and we made our way back to the edge of the stage. Pastor Donnie was welcomed back to the stage as the band commenced leading the next phase of the program. Purpose Life Church was the next on the program and they were welcomed by the audience with a great shout of praise. The ministry had a powerful mass choir with the leading of the woman of God, Sister Andrene Downie. She led them in a powerful performance to the song 'Alpha and Omega' by Israel and New Breed. I had to stand and applaud as they left the stage, not because of their choice of song that happened to be one of my favorites but because of the excellence and the intense manner of worship.

The MC thanked them and we were advised to make our way to the back center of the stage as we were next on the program. The applause subsided and the man of God announced "people of God welcome none other than Minister David Manner and the voices of First United youth choir". We entered the lavished stage and I took my position with total confidence and began to glorify the name of Jesus. I continued in the spirit of joy and spoke in an authoritative tone "Oh magnify the Lord with me, and let us exalt his name together". The audience began to lift their voices in worship and the atmosphere was set as I waited for the worshipers to settle down and began to introduce the song selection and the soloist. The band began to play and I was in total surrender to the Holy Ghost and began to direct under the anointing. Sis Destiny began to worship then went directly in an optimal soprano tune that led the audience into a great shout of praise at the power that erupted from the petite young woman; she sang with total surrender that kept the audience on their feet from beginning to end. We bowed in appreciation and left the stage and went back to our seats where we were stopped and congratulated by everyone with whom we came into contact.

The program was now at the final stage where the soloists were being called to the stage. I sat and waited for my name to be called and Pastor McClurkin lifted his voice in enthusiasm and began to introduce me. "Congregation" he announced "please put your hands together and make way for Brother David Manner, a young man with a very promising future"; "Saints I can see with the naked eye as well as in the spirit that there's a mighty call on his life". I lifted my voice and gave the Lord the highest praise "hallelujah to the King of Kings and the Lord of Lords", and then I thanked the man of God for his kind words and went directly into my piece. I was led by the spirit and went straight into an original piece that I wrote. I began to lift my voice and allowed the Lord to have His way as I ministered under the anointing and unction of the spirit. I closed out my song and the crowd lifted their voices in shouts of praise unto the Lord. I left the stage with a spirt of humility as I looked into the crowd and saw my father and Ma Anna standing with Apostle Edwards, Bishop Brown, and Elder Mike. I was genuinely grateful to God for His goodness toward me. The remaining performances were uplifting, with each person ministering at their peak. Pastor Donnie closed out with the last entry and brought the house down as he sang to the glory of God. The night came to an end and we made our way to the exit. Sister Kylee and Minister Daniel met us as we were leaving the building. "David" I was startled by the familiar voice of Pastor McClurkin and I immediately stopped and greeted him with a grin. He congratulated me once again while placing a business card in my hand and said "please call me ASAP as I have a proposal for you", then disappeared into the thick crowd. Daniel and Kylee looked at each other and screamed "yes" in unison; Kylee continued to speak "my bother" she continued in a meek tone "for I know the thoughts that I think toward you, says the Lord, thoughts of peace, and not evil, to give you an expected end". I smiled at her and continued to make my way out of the building and realized that Minister Alistair was in my peripheral view with a look of defeat.

Chapter 7

The week following the Gospel Fest was so surreal; life as I knew it had taken a significant turn and First United Choir was on the lips of those in Christendom. We were being raved about by Christian radio personalities and debut on the front cover of Gospel Today Magazine under the sub topic 'look out world'. This was a positive Christian magazine which was nationally known, which featured some of gospels most talented recording artists. This month's copy featured excellent men and women such as: Micah Stampley, Tejan Edwards, Sharee Williams, Byron Cage and Pastor Donnie McClurkin, just to name a few. Youth service on Friday night was more powerful than previous ones as the young people were on fire for God. The group was connecting on a deeper level in the spirit as we were hungry for souls and determined to win a city for the Kingdom. Sunday morning service was equally anointed and so was the moderator Minister Daniel. He was delighted to announce to the church, the choir's spectacular performance with the leading of Sister Destiny and myself in the solo performance. He concluded the update by saying "may I make a suggestion and feel free to say amen if you agree church";" who would love to see a collaboration of our own Sister Destiny and Brother David Manner?" The congregation went ballistic with amens and hallelujahs that brought a broad smile on Apostle Edwards' face. At the close of the service Pastor and First Lady Edwards handed out an envelope to each participant for their devotion to the ministry. Immediately following the service the congregation was invited to a lavish dinner in the multipurpose hall; the food and fellowship was much like the description of the scripture in Psalm chapter 133 that unity was exactly what was needed to make the move of God go in the direction of His glory.

I returned to work the following morning and my heart was overwhelmed to know that my father had lived up to his promise and had shown up at the concert. Andrea, my father's executive assistant met me at the entrance of the facility and greeted me with a cheerful embrace and congratulated me on my successful performance. I waved goodbye to Elder Mike and followed her to the elevator, where Andrea began to tell me of the goodness of the Lord as she held my hand and encouraged me. The elevator came to a stop at the executive floor and we exited with her still ministering to me in a motherly fashion. I walked into the extravagantly furnished room that never ceased to amaze me; the smell of the room was always captivating and inviting. I stood in the middle of the room secretly admiring every detail of the space: from the oversized French windows that gave the room its unique detail, the perfectly finished oak desk that hosted some of the most beautiful leather chairs I had ever seen with the naked eye, and the dark stained wood floor that complimented the beautiful art pieces that hung on the four corners of each wall. I smiled to myself and made a vow that I would someday own an office of the same magnitude but instead of expensive art work, mine would be more family oriented to give me the feel of having a home away from home at all times. "How are you" my father greeted interrupting my day dream. I turned and faced him with my eyes total fixated and his strong features that we both shared. He was professionally dressed in a black leather sport coat and an immaculate buttoned up white cotton shirt and navy slacks. I took another glance at his attire and smiled to myself as I saw so much of me in the figure standing before me. I caught myself and returned the greeting with a hearty hand shake. "I know we spoke over the phone but I just had a need to see you in person to congratulate you once again on the excellent performance of both you and that phenomenal choir. The event in all aspects was more than I'd expected and every item was breathtaking.

I hope you don't mind me putting in my reservation for next year right now". 'Ok' I thought to myself, 'I know I'm not dreaming', I chucked putting my right thumb up signifying 'just perfect'. "Have a seat" he instructed me, so I took the invitation as he sat directly across from me. He then reached across a vacant seat and stretched for his leather oversized briefcase and gently removed his copy of 'Gospel Today' magazine that featured me and our choir on the cover. He placed the magazine on his desk and spoke in a serious tone, "this is favor and I know you're already aware that God is working on your behalf. I'm very happy for you; there is no other way but up son, so keep focused and be yourself at all times". I agreed and sincerely thanked him for being present at the show. "David" he continued, "this isn't the only reason I asked to see you today. I believe you deserve a well overdue break so I'll be relieving you from all manual duties from this facility for thirty days". I was ecstatic to hear the words that came from his mouth and thought to myself that this was the perfect opportunity for me to prepare for the equivalency test to earn my high school diploma online. He them handed me a bulky sealed envelope and looked at me with a sly grin and teased "don't look so surprised, He is the God of the impossible, am I right?" "That He is" I responded. I knew that Andrea was making an impact on him and was thankful for the change of heart that had come. I placed the envelope in my pocket, exited the office, and made my way to the first floor making a much required stop. I knocked at the door of Elder Mike's office and awaited the invite; once in the room I gave him an update on all that had transpired with my dad and told him he had granted me a leave of absence that couldn't have come at a more convenient time. Mike got up from his desk and hugged me with joy and blessed me. I left the room and made my way to the basement, gathering all my miscellaneous items and placed them along with the packet that I'd receive in my backpack and secured them in my locker.

The next morning I woke up with joy in my heart knowing that I could worship the Lord a little longer and stay in His presence as He directed. I entered the washroom in the mindset of praise as I lifted my voice to the Holy God. I stepped out of the shower with great enthusiasm and closed out my time of consecration. I reached across the table and took my phone from my backpack. I scrolled down the call log and dialled Ma Anna from the list and alerted her that I was on my way. I closed the door of the cottage and walked leisurely, enjoying the scenery because despite the cold weather it was a beautiful day. I thanked the Lord for giving me the gift of life which made me appreciative to the fullest. Ma Anna stood on the porch with her tiny hands on both hips and a beautiful smile that could bring light to any dark place. Her presence inspired me so I quickened my steps to an almost jog and hugged her with great joy. She returned the gesture and with tears streaming down her face she inquired "how are you?", "I missed your presence more than words can express". I had spoken to her every chance I had during my absence and had shared all the relevant information, but the feeling was mutual as I shared the same sentiments. She opened the door that lead to her quarters in the great house, and told me to make myself comfortable. She left the room briefly and returned with a platter for two and began to serve the hefty meal which consisted of my favorite ackee and cod fish with sweet ripe plantains and golden fried dumplings. This must be Heaven I thought as Ma Anna definitely went over and beyond in preparing this meal. It was moments as these that I truly appreciated her culture; she was a native of the Island Jamaica and as they would say 'this woman can really tun har han an mek fashion'. She began to pour the rich cocoa tea in the two mugs that were already set at the table and told me to help myself to the French vanilla or caramel creamer and my choice of sweeteners. We ate leisurely, savoring every bite as I told her of every detail that happened in my absence; she listened with delight while making occasional comments to agree or encourage me. We ate our fill and she excused herself and returned with two servings of fresh fruits. She sat again and waited until I was finished eating then she looked me in my eyes with a smile on her face and said the words that would make my day even more blessed. "David the word of the Lord declares: if God is for you then who can be against you? You are blessed going out and blessed coming in and no weapon that is formed against you will ever be able to prosper". I thanked her for her words of blessing and teased her in my usual manner, "with words like these and meals as those you may be seeing me more often than usual; be careful now" I said and laughed until I nearly lost my balance from my chair. "Oh you're so funny" she giggled, you know you can be my guest of honor anytime. The vibration from my phone startled me and quickly I removed it from my jacket and answered the call. "Praise the Lord Jesus" I greeted the caller who was none other than Pastor Donnie McClurkin, "praise the Lord Brother David" he greeted with excitement, "thank you for accepting the offer, sorry it took me so long to return your call; I was in an early meeting, so how you have been? I see that you're doing as well as expected". "I'm blessed sir, truly the Lord has been good to me and I'm just humbled at the grace of Jesus over my life". "Awesome" he responded, and then continued the conversation, "are you ready for the next phase of your life Mr. Manner?"; "I am ready to offer you a recording contract, the ball is in your court, and the sky is the limit". I was more than willing to plunge right into this offer as the timing was great and I knew that my music would be able to reach those who wouldn't otherwise be able to hear it. I listened as he made the proposal with a contented heart glorifying my Savior and Lord. "Are you there" his voice came through with a ring; "I'm sorry" I responded "yes I am, it was just taking me a minute to process but yes, yes and yes to all the above". We spoke for a few more minutes then closed out the conversation with a verbal agreement of me accepting the recording contract and ready to go to new horizons. Ma Anna waited earnestly as I hung up the phone; she smiled at me and I noticed the tears that began to freely flow. She placed her finger on her lips and uttered "no worries son these are tears of joy, solely tears of joy".

I made my way to the backside of the property and realized that the day had warmed up to a much more bearable temperature. I made myself as comfortable as could be and removed my phone from my pocket; I uttered a brief prayer and began to make the much needed call. "Shalom my beloved", Evangelist Kylee greeted. "Shalom my beloved" I responded, "how are you little bro" she teased" getting much needed rest I hope", "yes" I responded "a little more for the time being". "However" I continued "that might change in a little while", "why is that?" she inquired, "what are you up to David Manner?" she spoke in a stern tone. "Don't go over the edge mother hen" I teased, "oh no you didn't go there" she laughed "yes I did" I defended, "ok mister I'll let you get away this time" Kylee laughed "only you or Daniel is allowed to use that term loosely because I will admit you are my chickens". I sighed and hesitated briefly "I have some information to share, are you all ears mother hen?" I teased. "Yes I am" she said changing her tone to sound more dignified, "ok here goes, I got a phone call today from Pastor Donnie", "you did" she interrupted and continued "well go ahead", her tone was more excited as she hastened me. "Ok" I continued sarcastically, "well he offered me a record deal and he's ready for me to get to work ASAP". Kylee began to glorify God both through tears and laughter. "David" she screamed "are you for real beloved?" "Yes I am big sis, yes I am"; "hold the line baby brother" she instructed and the phone was silent for a brief moment then I heard a male voice that I quickly identified as Daniel's. "David" Kylee sobbed "Daniel is on the line, I told him of what happened"' he also lifted his voice in prayer and began to give the Lord thanks for the doors that He was opening and those that were being closed. I hung up the call with a new found confidence knowing and realizing that Jesus Christ was my Alpha and Omega; He had provided for me in ways that seemed impossible. Daniel and Kylee were no different to me than natural siblings and I knew that the Lord had designed my life in this fashion even before the foundation of the world; truly I was blessed and highly favored. I continued to make the necessary phone calls: first to Elder Michael followed by Destiny, then concluded with a call to Apostle Edwards. I updated them on all that had transpired on the phone meeting with Pastor McClurkin. I knew that I had a responsibility as a sheep to be submissive to the shepherd. There was one final call on my agenda but somehow I was apprehensive in dialling the number. I inhaled then exhaled then inhaled and exhaled and eventually the situation didn't seem as hard as before. The phone rang and with my thoughts being as clear as crystal I was ready for whatever was before me. "Manner enterprise and equipment Andrea speaking", "praise the Lord Sister Andrea this is David, how are you?", "I'm well" she replied in her usual energetic tone. "How is your first day off?", "God is awesome" I stated "I'm doing as well as expected", "amen" she responded, "that's just the goodness of Jesus, I guess you didn't call to chit chat with me she laughed, I'll put your dad on the line, you timed him well as he just wrapped up a general meeting with the board of directors; I'll put you through to his private line, hang on a bit and God bless you in all your endeavors". I thanked her and waited on the line as the soft jazz tune played. "Hi David" my father greeted me in a soft tone "you needed to speak to me, are you ok?" he inquired. "Hi" I responded "yes all is well, I just needed to share a bit of news with you", "ok great" he responded in an eager tone "go ahead". I continued to speak sharing with my father everything from receiving the business card to the previous phone call that I received from Pastor McClurkin and the offer of the record contract. "I just wanted to make you aware of the direction I have decided to take in the next phase of my life"; "I have so much that I need to accomplish and I just need your support with these critical changes". He listened in silence then spoke in an apologetic tone "son you have all the support you need, I'm here if you should ever need me"; his voice began to crack as he added his last statement, "thank you son for sharing your plans with me, this is more than I expected of you but never the less, thank you". I assured him that I wouldn't have it any other way and blessed him as I concluded the call.

The day was still young and there was so much I had to give the Lord thanks for so I closed my eyes and went to the secret place in the Holy Spirit; I needed to loose myself in His anointing. 'How glorious is our God' I thought; we had the privilege to enter into His throne room freely to offer up sacrifices of praise. I began to worship Him in spirit and in truth as I waited to be led in the most holy place. I released my heart and followed the Lord on the journey He was taking me; a new path where I surrendered my all and be still and know that He is God. He was now ready to release me to new horizons and higher levels in His manifold blessings.

The week following turned out to be more than I expected. Ma Anna and I spent every morning dining and catching up on the things of God and His goodness toward us. I laid in my room after leaving the main house and began to go through the brochure in the package that Daniel had shared with me previously. The packet contained information on how to acquire a high school diploma in an accelerated time online. I scrolled through the pages with joy knowing that the time was right. The phone rang and the caller ID signified that the caller was Pastor Donnie, "praise the Lord Pastor" I greeted, "bless the Lord he responded, I hope you had enough time to let my proposal soak in". "Yes"

I assured him and we went on to speak in detail of all that was expected of me in preparation for signing as a recording artist. We wrapped up the phone call with the agreement of meeting in his studio in a few days.

Daniel and Kylee sat in their vehicle and waited as I made my way to meet them at the entrance of the driveway. Ma Anna was sitting on the front porch and as I approached she hugged me and handed me a bag, "well you'll be eating on the run again mister, so here you go". I took the package from her and held her hands as I headed to the driveway. "Ma Anna" I spoke as I approached the SUV "these are my dear friends that I told you about, Daniel and Kylee"; they both exited the vehicle as I introduced them to each other formally and they embraced joyfully. Ma Anna blessed the two young people and thanked them for being a source of support for me and encouraged them that their kindness hadn't gone unnoticed as God was their rewarder. We waved goodbye to her and left on the journey which according to our navigation was a twenty five minute ride to the studio. We pulled up to the studio a few minutes earlier than the estimated time. Daniel drove into the parking lot and Kylee prayed our final prayer before making our way into the building. The security checked our identification and approved our entry to the facility. I approached the front desk and introduced myself to the young lady who was awaiting my arrival. She directed us to the studio and congratulated me as being the newest artist. I was impressed at the anointing in the building; the presence of the Lord was surely evident in the atmosphere. Pastor Donnie was anticipating our arrival and met us at the door, "come on in" he smiled, "how was the journey?" Daniel responded and informed him that the trip was easier than expected. He invited us into his office that was adjacent to the recording room. I began the process of signing the necessary documents before heading to the studio. We concluded the signing and I entered the sound booth and went into full gear. The engineer began to play the track and the anointing took total control of me as flesh had to be completely diminished. I began to minister the first song and the words were smoother than ever before. I lifted my voice as the presence of the Lord filled the room taking me beyond the veil. I closed my eyes in total surrender allowing the Holy Spirit to move freely on this first recording knowing that everything was in His hand from this day forward. I followed the queues as Pastor Donnie instructed and sang as the music came through the speakers. The recording lasted for about an hour then I was directed to exit the glass proof area; the smiles were apparent on each of my audiences face as Pastor Donnie began to congratulate me once again for a job well done. I left the studio that day giving glory to Jesus who was my help every step of the way; the spirit made it clear to my mind that there was no stopping from this point forward.

We drove back to the house and discussed how the word of God could never return void unto Him but accomplish that which it was sent out to do. I got to my destination and thanked both Daniel and Kylee for their continued support and made my way to the end of the property to my cottage. Once inside I fell before the Lord in total reverence of His goodness towards me. Life will throw its punches, but my life was evident of the mercies of God when you wait on him. The Lord will open the portals and move obstacles that blocks blessings. Jesus was able to slay all the giants that comes to kill, steal, or destroy. Today was the first day of my new life as a recording artist and I was ready to go wherever life took me.

CHAPTER 8

The Sunday morning service was at its best as the anointing was in full flow. Pastor Edwards stood in the pulpit and allowed the Lord to have His way. He waited for the opportune time and when the spirit allowed him to move forward he called my name and gestured for me to join him. I approached the pulpit as the man of God spoke lifting his voice "beloved brother and sister please make way for gospel recording artist and the newest edition to McClurkin House, our own David Manner". I pointed my finger to the heaven and spoke in a voice of humility "all glory to God saints, to Him be all honor and praise". "Amen" declared Pastor Edwards and he continued to address the congregation, "church this young man has a story to tell and he is determined to use his music to win souls. He has been called to minister to the Kingdom in such a time as this and he is determined to fulfill his promise to reach out to whosoever will. Our God is no respecter of person's saints, His promises are always sure. I think I've said enough" he said. "Just one more thing before I hand over to him; his new release is available for purchase today". He handed me the mic and smiled at me as he left the podium encouraging me saying "speak as you're led son". "Praise the Lord family, I think Pastor had done enough for both of us so I will be very brief before you. I just want to give honor to my Lord and Savior Jesus Christ who is the head of my life; He is great and does all things in His own time. Today I must encourage you that there is no one like our God. I would also like to give special thanks to Elder Mike, Missionary Fraser and their children, my inherited family; none of this would have been possible had he not extended me an invitation to the youth revival that led to this point. Also I want to extend thanks to Minister Daniel and Evangelist Kylee for being ever present in my time of need; these two young people cleared their schedules and was there for moral support on my first project. Church I continued the journey which has been nothing short of a blessing. God has not forgotten any of you; let your request be known unto Him that is faithful to perform it to the end. Please pray my strength as my determination is to go all the way in God". I handed the mic to Pastor Edwards and reclaimed my seat at the keyboard. I felt peace of mind as these people were my family; I was loved and warmly received from the first time I walked through the doors of this building.

My desire was to serve God's children and I was exactly where I needed to be at this point in my life. I walked out of the Sanctuary shortly after the close of the service and met Sister Destiny who wore the most beautiful smile I'd ever seen on anyone. She greeted me with a hug that made my heart leap with joy; she had always been able make me smile even on my worst days. I took my assigned seat at the table that was beautifully decorated by Abigail and Kylee; the ladies had done a phenomenal job in displaying the CD with my new single. The saints began to surround me and as was expected all the CD's were sold within the hour. I thanked the ladies for their support and made my way to the parking lot with Elizabeth, Hannah, and Abbey. Elder Mike and Missionary Fraser were patiently waiting for us to journey home. Upon arrival, I opened my bedroom door and began to undress from my church attire when I was interrupted by a knock on the door. "David" Elder Mike called, "dinner is served". I quickly washed my hands and face then made my way back to the dining room. "Surprise" the voices yelled as I entered the room; my eyes popped out as Pastor Edwards and First Lady Edwards along with their children Joshua, Anna, and the entire choir stood in the gigantic kitchen and dining area of the house. The bell rang again and this time Elder and Evangelist Johnson made appearance along with

Minister Daniel and Kylee. Minister Onajhe, Evangelist Ashley, and Destiny came in directly afterward and guest after guest continued to make their appearance. It was now evident to me why the food on the Island looked enough to feed an army. The curried goat was mouth-watering, the side of roast was beautifully glazed and ready to be devoured. There was enough jerk and fried chicken to feed the multitude and the side dishes consisted of two of my favorites: perfectly seasoned potato salad and creamy Coleslaw. I was ready to eat but Missionary Fraser raised the upbeat tune "for he's a jolly good fellow, yes he's a jolly good fellow, for he's a jolly good fellow and so says all of us"; everyone had now joined in the chorus and sang toghther with great joy. My heart was rejoicing and I began to silently thank God for His blessing and thought to myself 'only He can do all things well'. All the guests were now seated as prior arrangement was made to accommodate everyone. Elder Mike announced in a still soft voice "let us pray"; the words of the prayer was sincere, touching me to the very core. He thanked the Lord for allowing him the privilege to be my mentor and for blessing him with a son who was humble in more ways than one. His prayer was brief but every word was ushered from the very depth of his soul. He closed out by sanctifying the food and announced "let's eat". Everyone began to fill their plates and the celebration took off in full gear. Destiny took the cordless mic and announce above the voices "ladies and gentlemen, boys and girls, I greet you all in the mighty name of Jesus. We are gathered here today in honor of our friend, our brother, and even son to some; none other than our beloved David". Everyone began to lift their voices in a solemn 'amen'. "Saints the mic is open to those who would like to make a toast for Brother David's accomplishment in honor of his new CD release". Kylee was the first to approach the mic, she cleared her throat and with her hands lifted she spoke in an enthusiastic tone. "Please lift your glasses of sparkling cider to my baby brother who has stood the test and has proven that paradox that no matter what storm cloud-God will. May the Lord continue to use you my beloved, the best is yet to come". The toasts came one after another, with each person thanking the Lord for His blessing on my life. Sis Destiny handed the mic to Missionary Fraser, "can I have everyone's attention one last time" she announced. "Amen" we chorused, as she continued to speak in her usual soft tone "I just want to bless the Johnsons and Heavenly Delights for catering the food before us. It's truly a taste of heavenly delights and I know we can all attest to that", "yes" everyone agreed in unison and baby Anna Christina jumping up and down "yes heavenly" she mimicked; we all laughed at her usual way of having the last say. "Ok miss Anna you have said it well" missionary Fraser giggled.

It had been a little over a year that God had predestined for me to meet my beloved father figure and mentor Elder Michael Fraser. We took a single look at each other and immediately our spirits connected, creating a bond. He was informed by Andrea, my father's executive assistant that I was his new intern; I can remember her spoken words in my mind as if it was yesterday. "Mike this is David Manner, yes David Manner! Please take him to the lower level and get him started right away. Mike, she repeated, this is a very extraordinary young man and I know you will take him as your own". She then turned away and left us; her intense words riveted in both our hearts. Mike smiled at me and assured me that everything would be ok. That was the first day of the rest of my new found life as he was more than a son could ever ask for; we have been inseparable from that day onward. My own father had never allowed me to leave the property until I met this humble man of God; he invited me to the meeting that would change the course of my life. I walked into the revival on the first night and realized that the Lord had predestined this friendship even before the very foundation. My pastor and his wife were the most loving and transparent people I'd ever met; they were nothing short of a blessing to my life from the very first day I met then up to this point. Mr. and Mrs. Johnson were totally a blessing along with their children Kylee and Daniel. I took a deep look at my surroundings and was overjoyed that everyone was in fellowship in honor of my life and all that the Lord bestowed on me.

I walked across the room and entered the kitchen and began to refill my glass with the freshly made fruit juice that was provided by Sister Cleo who was lovingly known by everyone as Aunty Cleo. She made the best mouth-watering drink on this side of glory. Sister Cleo was a petite and beautiful woman, the mother of two sons the older was Giovani and the younger was Kymani. Daniel who was best friend with her youngest was often provided with bottles of the signature beverage that he would unselfishly share on occasions with me. I could never get accustomed to the refreshing taste of this drink as I poured a second glass. I took another gulp and was about to take another when I was greeted by a melodious voice; "I see you're getting the most of Aunty Cleo's drink; well we know that at least one person would endorse her if she ever decides to market this product". I smiled at her admiring her sweet sense of humor. "Are you enjoying the party?" she inquired; I looked at her in disbelief and answered in a sarcastic tone, "are you serious with that rhetorical question? What is there not to enjoy? You guys throw the best events ever". "Ok" she agreed "true! First United got it on lock, you said it" I shook my head in agreement. "So what is your next move" she continued, "Should I have a next move?", "oh I'm sorry" she began to apologize, "I'm kidding" I said, "no need for apologies"; "my next step is to finish this project; the completion of an album with all original materials that were written in my time of consecration before the Sovereign God". We continued to share our goals and desires and came to the same conclusion that our reason for living was solely to worship the Lord and live our lives to please Him.

The guests began to depart but not before each person congratulated me on allowing the Lord to move in my life. We all chipped in and helped Mrs. Fraser to get the house back in order. I walked back to my room and fell before the Lord with tears of joy streaming down my face. I began to exalt the name of the Lord Jesus Christ and bless Him for his mighty works. I woke up the next morning still basking in the glory of the Risen Savior. I made my way to the shower and began to prepare for the day ahead. I turned on the pipe with the rain shower head and immediately I was back in full harmony, singing songs of praises to my God. I got dressed and straightened my room making it fit for a king, then proceeded to the living area. Mrs. Fraser was sitting at the Island and greeted me with her usual cheery voice "well good morning my good man, I'm happy you've decided to join me; have seat and make yourself comfy" she stated. I smiled and greeted her with a bright "good morning and bless the Lord mother, I'll be happy to join you". The sweet smell of chocolate and cinnamon saturated the room; I poured a cup of the hot delicious beverage and helped myself to a serving of fluffy pancakes and golden scrambled eggs along with a few slices of turkey bacon; I blessed my food and began to indulge. I was in the middle of the meal when Mrs. Fraser called my name in a motherly tone, "David, how is your studies coming along?" she inquired. I knew she was speaking of the high school equivalency test that I was scheduled to take shortly. I answered her with a burst of confidence and assured her that it was going as good as expected; "no worries" I said "I know God's got it and I'm going to knock this one at the top of the scoreboard". She chuckled and shook her head, unable to respond to my funny sense of humor. It was winding down to the close of my vacation so I spent the remaining days in extreme studying, gearing up for the exam. Minister Daniel would visit me from time to time, quizzing and preparing me in the best way possible. The test date came and did extremely excellent and even exceeded Daniel's expectations. I was definitely on the right path; nowhere but up from here! I was determined to stay in the perfect will of God. With exactly one week to conclude my month of leave, I was ready to return to the studio to complete the unfinished work on my project. The Lord had dropped the name of the album in my spirit and I believe that it says everything that represents me and my life; the name of the project was 'From Defeat to Victory'.

The recording sessions were amazing and the anointing was evident on each track. I walked out from the booth at the completion of yet another great accomplishment and Pastor Donnie was standing there to meet me. He held out his hand and shook mine as he beamed with excitement and said, "things are definitely looking great, you are getting to higher heights and deeper depths in every session and I love the intimacy between you and the Holy Spirit. I believe that this album will reap an abundance of souls that has never been touched before; this is definitely headed for a Grammy" he spoke with surety. "We have been experiencing immense testimonies. I heard that during the recording sessions many of the engineer's lives has literally taken a turn; I for one can't wait to put out this project". I looked at the man of God as he spoke with enthusiasm and waited for him to breathe, then I spoke in a humble and sincere tone. "Pastor, it was never ever a plan of mine to be in a studio ministering these songs but I will adhere to the voice of God and let His will be done". I lifted my voice and continued to express my take on what was said; I continued "I guess the Lord will use a mess to send His message, or a sad story for His divine glory, and I for one know what it takes to let self be slain for His gain". He looked at me with joy and asked "is that the title for our next track?" I looked back at him with my face held straight and replied "thou knowest", we both broke out in a loud uproar and laughed like I'd never laughed in a long time. He straightened his shirt and continued "ok let's get to back to business". He was trying to keep a straight face, then said "David, I believe were going to need a female voice to collaborate on the final song: 'Lord you're worthy oh so worthy' ok young man?" I was taken aback because the same thought visited my mind at least twice and on both occasions Sister Destiny came before me.

I looked at him and shook my head in agreement, "so it's a thought then?" he reiterated "yes it is" I agreed.

Pastor Edwards picked me up from the studio that day. I stepped in the car in high spirits and a joyful mood due to the great news that I had just received. We greeted each other and began our journey. "You seem very happy, you're all smiles" he said and looked at me briefly then turned his focus back to the road; "Yes sir" I answered hurriedly "ok" he said keeping his focus ahead "well do you care to share or is it personal? If so, I wouldn't want to pry". "Oh no sir, you wouldn't be prying at all and I would love to share my blessing with you". I explained everything that had transpired in the studio, telling him how the man of God, Pastor Donnie had pitched an idea that was in my mind for the longest and somehow I believe that the Lord had shared my unspoken word. "Well, He has been known to do as such" he interjected. I enlighten him that I was now narrowing down to the final track on the album when he pitched the idea of collaborating with a female on the song; "That's great" he laughed, "so did you have anyone in mind?" I laughed and continued to speak in confidence "well I thought the Lord would reveal the rest of His plans as He has done a great job thus far". "Amen, I hear you" Pastor joked "don't be like that David, He does all things for our good", "indeed He does" I agreed. "Sir I had already thought this through one too many times and I'm fully convinced that Sister Destiny James would complement the song to a perfect T and take this song to the core of perfection. She has a way of delivering with power that can change the course of nature. I pray it wouldn't be too much to ask for her support on this final song". He looked at me with nothing short of gratitude in his eyes and began to commend me of being very thoughtful. "David" he sighed, "I believe the Lord has definitely spoken to you; you couldn't have been more correct in your choice, this young lady is not only an excellent minister but she is a well-polished child of God. I believe she would be honored to do this project with you".

The phone call to Destiny was very intense but I became more relaxed as I shared the news with her. She listened in silence as I told her how important it was to me to have her use her gift to collaborate with me. I paused and began to silently pray with the hope that she would accept the proposal; the silence was broken when she screamed with joy and spoke "David Manner I hope you're not playing a prank on me mister", I assured her I was as serious as a judge. I updated her on the date and time of the next recording and we ended the conversation on an oral agreement. My life had taken a supernatural turn for the best. Destiny and I met at Elder Mike's home to practice for a few hours; the song was quickly perfected, indicating that the lyrics was definitely written for two. We traveled together to the studio and ministered the song in the fullness of the spirit. Pastor Donnie was ecstatic and praised God for my quick response to the proposal. I thank the Lord for being in total control as He never seizes to amaze me of His grace on my life; all I had to do was let go and let God have His way. I began to reflect on the words of a very wise lady, my dear Ma Anna who often ministered to me saying 'as long as the agape love was abiding in me, the presence of the Lord will always abide with me'. I was living my dream of being a servant of God and many had repented of their sins and took on the name of Jesus through water baptism. I was humbled to see how the Lord was allowing me to become a fisher of men.

The phone rang and it was Pastor McClurkin reminding me of the schedule for my last appointment. I was anticipating this day like none other, knowing that Destiny was going to be with me. I hurried to the shower and lifted my voice to the Lord in consecration as I prepared myself to meet with her. I opened the door of the walk-in closet and pulled out a stack of freshly laundered clothes. I selected a tailored designer black slacks and a navy blue blazer matching it nicely with a white polo shirt. I bushed my hair to perfection and made my way to the kitchen; I was surprised by Kylee and Destiny. Kylee was having a cup of cappuccino with Mrs. Fraser, "good morning" I greeted the ladies as I sat and poured myself a cup of hot water and added some lemon juice and began to sip the hot beverage. Look who decided to join us "mother hen, I mean Kylee" I teased. I smiled but kept silent "so now cats got your tongue?" Destiny joked "I pray they'll loosen it by the time we get to our destination". I laughed at her humor but still didn't respond. Mrs. Fraser left the room and returned with a bottle of consecrated oil and pronounced a blessing upon us for journeying mercies, which was followed by a prayer of unmerited favor on Destiny and me from Sister Kylee. The drive to the studio was spent in worship as we started listening to the single of my new release from Brooklyn all the way to Long Island. Destiny sat at the rear of the vehicle and lifted her voice with the music. We walked through the security check and proceeded straight into the building and headed to the studio; we were half an hour before our scheduled appointment. Pastor Donnie was a man of an excellent spirit so I'd made being early my point of duty.

Destiny was observing her surroundings being her usual self in the spirit of meekness. I introduced her to Pastor Donnie who in turn introduced her to the entire team. We were offered two cups of lemon tea by his assistant, Sister Klonde and all I could say was 'perfect'. We sipped slowly as we listened to his the final instructions. We entered the sound booth, placed our head phones over our heads, and waited for the cue from the engineer. He signaled us and we went directly into the bridge, followed by Sister Destiny with first verse. We collaborated on the chorus followed by me on the second verse. The power of God filled the room and Pastor Donnie was in total worship as we sang to the glory of God. We went to a second and a third take, and at this point everyone under the sound of our voice was soaked in the anointing. We walked out of the sound booth glorifying the name of Jesus. The man of God embraced both Destiny and I and declared that we both outdid ourselves. He continued to bless us with words of encouragement. He spoke in a tone of surety and declared "God trusted you with a message to His people and you delivered this album on point; there no doubt a harvest of souls will be reaped through this project". I looked at him and spoke audibly "where He leads I will follow". He hugged Destiny and spoke in the prophetic, "young lady you have a very bright future ahead of you, see you at the finish line; the hand of God is upon you". We walked up to Kylee who was still basking in the glory of God; she hugged us and we broke out in praise once more. I was overwhelmed and all I wanted to do at this moment was to hold my dear beloved Ma Anna, because I knew she was praying for me.

Chapter 9

I walked to the backside of the property with the thought of reconnecting with the place where it had all started. I was sold on the fact that one should never forget humble beginnings. I pierced my eyes looking unto the hills on the things above and glorified the Lord just for who He is. Everything was as I'd last seen them, truly this was my sacred place; I thanked God for allowing my eyes to see Him in all things. I took my spot on the best seat in the house, and indeed it was 'my smooth rock'. The rock was all that was required to keep me still in His presence. I sat in awe of the scenery as my heart reconnected in a way that made my soul become more aware of the blessed hope. The sweet fragrance of spring ignited the air; the stream was flowing in perfection as the ducks swam in pairs nonchalantly. The spirit was thick around me and I wanted to let go of everything that would hinder my mind from touching my God. I closed my eyes and disconnected my thoughts from my will as I began to offer up a sacrifice the Lord most holy. Souls were being saved by the minute as the album had taken wings of its own and all the promises of God were proven to be sure. I had seen the move of God on my generation and had submitted to His will once more. The glory of the Lord was evident all around me as I began to thank Him for His guidance and His direction on my new horizon. I began to weep in His presence for His mighty acts and His marvelous works. I was happy to be at one on this intimate level once again and I felt with all my heart that He had ushered me back to Him because he was also longing to meet me in this place. He began to fill me with a new passion and anoint me at a level that was deeper than I'd experience in my absence; I began to magnify Him from my innermost being and the words of new songs began to flow from my soul. With my voice lifted, I sang with a new level of anointing. "How great my Lord is, how true is your love towards us, Lord we surrender our hearts, our mind, our will, take me Lord, all of me, I surrender my all". I continued to worship in the beauty of holiness and it was evident that I had surrendered my will and my way. God had opened the windows of heaven over me, allowing me to see beyond the veil. The man Abraham was faithful in all things whether it was his tithe or time and I was determined to follow in the ways of the men of old.

My life had accelerated at a pace beyond my expectation but my time with God, I knew was priceless. I was now lying prostrate before the Lord as He ministered to my soul; time was not important and as for food, I was filled in Him because in Him all things were complete. I awoke and began to lift my almost lifeless body from the grass that had cushioned me; my surroundings had receded from light to the setting of the sun beyond the horizon. The Lord had proved once again that He was my portion; I entreated of the Holy Spirit and He answered me. I began to minister the word of truth to everyone, telling those who were willing to listen about the good news. It was a proven fact that when you seek ye first the kingdom of God and His righteousness, everything else will be added to you. I had begun this journey with a less than promising future but my commitment to His will had now profited me in the overflow. I was now sought after by some of the best Universities and I knew that I was nothing short of His benefits; this was truly a season of blessed proportions. I was no longer employed by Manner Enterprises as my father had taken the initiative to release me from my duties and had blessed me generously. My life as a gospel recording artist was one that was demanding yet satisfying. Pastor McClurkin was a true mentor and a humble man of God who had unselfishly shared the expertise of the music business, withholding nothing.

I was living in God's abundant blessing and I never for a moment reflected on my humble beginning and thought that I would ever require professionals to direct me in different aspects of my career; but life has proved otherwise. I was now assigned a manager who would advise me concerning my day to day operation and also an accountant to navigate me in handling my finances. I was a firm believer in the blessings of God and the knowledge of His faithfulness; when God begins to pour out His blessings, He will take you to places you've never imagined. Job is an example of one who experienced new horizons; he trusted in the Lord without reservation and was rewarded with a double portion. My life was not as rigorous as the man Job, but like me, I know many could compare their lives to some elements of his. There were many things that were delayed in my life; some were more anticipated than others, even though I yearned for a number of unsurfaced wishes. I was encouraged by the thought that delays were never meant to be denials; my life had taken for the most part a three hundred and sixty degree turn. I was at the highest point in my natural life but there were still decisions that had to be made cornering my change.

I made my way back to the small cottage and picked up my phone and begun to make the call that I had procrastinated to make for the last two months. "David" my father answered the phone after two short rings "how are you?", "I'm blessed and you?" I inquired, "I'm doing well, God is good". I had rehearsed this conversation so many times in my head but everything was now erased from my memory so I concluded that I had no other choice but to speak from the top of my head. 'Well here goes nothing' I thought as I proceeded, "dad" I continued as diplomatic as I could, "my life has taken a turn as you are most likely aware and I believe the time has come for me to make the transition concerning where I will be living from now on". "I can't say this has come as a total shock to me after all you have dealt with, being somewhat of an outcast and yet you've never once acted out of character; I will respect any decision you make". I thanked him for his continued support then ended the phone call; well that wasn't as hard as I thought and everything was going according to plan. The tiny room was almost completely empty and I began to reminisce on my life there. Ma Anna was a God-sent who had made every effort to bless me on every occasion. I will deeply regret being around her, along with my absence from the back end of the property where Jesus lived. Leaving from this place is definitely a tough but necessary decision.

Anna was waiting for me at the main house the following morning and ushered me in the house at my very sight. The sweet smell of apple cinnamon filled the atmosphere as I followed her into the massive front entrance where the high ceilings made the house look even bigger than it actually was. I began to admire the exclusiveness of this mansion with the beautiful spiral staircase that lead to the main living space. I continued to follow her into the grand kitchen and took a seat at the beautiful Granite Island as she poured me a cup of hot cocoa. I looked at her and my heart was warmed with her effortless ways of being completely generous to every person she was blessed to cross path with. I knew my phone call had brought her to the realization that my season here was over and the Lord had taken control of my life. I began to sip the warm beverage as the questions that I'd plan to asked her was now a thing of the past; all I wanted to do was enjoy the company of this very special woman. We spent the entire day enjoying each other's company as she tried her best to steer me in life's path as a man who was on his way to greatness. I left her and went back to my cottage with a peace of mind and indeed my sleep was sweet.

The morning air was deliciously sweet on this end of the property. I was relaxing after my morning worship when I heard a soft knock on the door. I looked out only to see Elder Mike standing there. He greeted me with a wide smile and waited for me to pass him my bags that had been previously packed. He humbly told me to take my time as he'll be waiting at the car. I closed the door and headed to the stream where I immediately removed my phone from my backpack and began to capture the beautiful scenery. This held a special place in my heart as it was the very place where many of the songs I wrote was birthed; this part of my life's journey was at a close. I lifted a final prayer to the Lord and thanked Him for allowing me to see Him in His fullness. I promised Him that I will always be in His submissive will. I walked by the cottage and continued to the entrance of the property and saw Ma Anna standing at the door. She appeared as one deep in thought as she gazed at the rose bushes; she smiled at my very presence and walked to meet me halting my final step. We hugged each other in a final embrace as the tears streamed from our eyes as a fountain; my heart was broken in so many places but at the same time I was happy to embrace the new phase. I thought to myself 'what an oxymoron'; I was experiencing my happiest and saddest moment all at once. We finally came to a place of composure and said our goodbyes with the promise to never let life separate us or to become strangers. I drove away from the place I'd called home and ventured on the journey of new beginnings; the duration of the journey was spent in utter silence.

I was greeted with warmth as I entered my new home; this was definitely a new dimension. Elder Mike held my hand to assure me that all was well. I thanked him for his continued support and his consistent generosity toward me. Mrs. Fraser hugged me and agreed with her husband that it was going to be ok. "David" she smiled as she offered her support "son you are home". I was ignited with a new release that felt as natural as the air we breathe. I walked to the area of the house where my once temporary and now permanent room was. I exhaled as I looked up to the Heavens and adored the Lord for His faithfulness. I unpacked my bags and made myself as comfortable as possible and began to process the thought 'home sweet home'. I must have been asleep for a lengthy time because the sun had begun to set as I rubbed my eyes and began to unwind; it was yet another Friday evening which meant we would be heading to youth service. I hurried to the shower as I remembered the words of warning from Liz and Abbey 'do not stall'. We arrived at the Church and made our way to the altar as it was our custom to be at one with God through intersession before each service. Sis Destiny took her position on the pulpit and began to lead with in-depth worship; the voices in the atmosphere was like the sound of an angelic choir as she serenaded her King to Martha Munizzi's 'I was created to make your praise glorious'. We were soaked in the anointing as the words of the song became alive in our souls and everyone in the sanctuary was bringing life to the scripture 'let everything that has breath praise ye the Lord'. We were like the wheat in the field on a spring day expressing gratitude to the most high God. She was now joined by the worship team Ariana, Abigail, Hannah and Liz who were among the group of worshippers. The atmosphere was now fully charged as we waited for the rain; the latter and the former rain together.

Sister Kylee took her place as the moderator; the power of God that was upon her was almost uncontainable. She began to sing the chorus of the final song with her eyes closed throughout as she abode in the realm of the spirit. She opened her eyes after a few moments and sent up a sacrifice of praise to the Lord. Abigail was called to lead the opening prayer and the Holy Ghost filled the room once again. I began to lift my voice in praise in an effort to allow the anointing to continue to rest on me; God had called me from my mother's womb and had destined me to this house. Today my heart was singing glory be to the Risen King. The course of the service was like none that we had experience in the past; old and young were led to realize that the room was transformed into the most holy place. Minister Onajhe was the one to exalt for the night's service and he was gifted as a teacher who was known to exegete any text that even a child would be able to comprehend. He spoke from the scripture Hebrew 4:12. I began to magnify the Lord in private knowing that there was going to be a mighty move of God; he began to read the scripture in sincerity as one who adobe in the secret place of the Most High. He continued by praying fervently to the Lord as it was his usual practice to ask the Lord to touch the hearts and mind of every person under the sound of his voice. The word came forth with power and clarity and bought us all to our knees; even those who were visiting among us were changed forever. He closed out the spoken word and handed me the mic as the anointing filled the room. I accepted the mic and lifted my voice, humbling myself in submission to the sovereign Lord as I entered the throne room. I began to minister and was taken to an altitude of worship.

Each day was absolutely a joy as my life as a psalmist meant that I was privileged to reach an otherwise unreachable generation, whether it was by appearing on Christian network that was viewed worldwide or being interviewed on national radio broadcast. These appearances were a means to minister and testify to those who needed to be encouraged and accept Jesus Christ as their Savior and Lord. Each moment was more humbling than the previous; I was blessed to know that the Lord could trust to use me in this fashion. My schedule was fully booked as I was called to minister in different arenas alongside some of gospels greatest. I was signed to McClurkin House and this meant that I was booked to capacity. The power of God was doing a mighty work though the music that the Lord had inspired me to write. Truly one had to be in a state of brokenness and dismay to understand what it meant to be pulled out from defeat to victory.

I began to bond with my father and our relationship was at a new height. I had longed to be a part of his life as a son for as long as I could remember. I am truly aware of my duty as a child of God to love him beyond the flesh and now was the time for me to prove the agape love in me. Destiny had become a great support not only as a partner on stage but had also proven herself to be a sister and a friend. I was able to express my deepest concerns or doubts to her. I knew that Ma Anna was missing in the flesh but her prayers were coming to fruition each day. I would make it my point of duty to connect with her spiritually at the beginning of each rising day; everything was like a blossom that budded into a beautiful flower.

Chapter 10

The summer heat was warm on my skin and as much as spring was always my favorite time of year, this season was quickly changing my mindset. What was meant by summer was not the intense heat or any contributing factor to the climate, it was now summarized to me as the season for extensive soul saving. The days were longer and this meant that the basketball courts would be grossly overcrowded, the fast food restaurants would be packed, and the community parks were almost filled to capacity daily. Young and old were basking in the pleasure that the longer days permitted them to take advantage of the outdoors. This was the opportune time for those of us that were hungry for souls to reap the benefits of the season and to evangelize overtime. Many of us only used that term when we are expecting monetary payment for labor or time that we have sacrificed for the reason of self-satisfaction or gratification; but to the laborers in the vineyard, it meant spiritual increase. The youth revival was fast approaching and my heart was rejoicing; we were all anticipating a mighty move of God once more. This year's lineup was expected to touch Heaven and change the lives of many who are pregnant with purpose. The speakers included great men of God such as Bishop TD Jakes, Apostle Charles Williams, Bishop Wayne Brown and our own Minister Onajhe Morgan, who was now promoted to youth pastor. Each speaker was truly equipped with the unique anointing to break yokes and remove burdens. The event would not be at its pinnacle without the ministry of the psalmist that would break fetters and chains to allow the power of God to manifest; the musical line up was just as powerful in terms of anointing. The items on the agenda for the revival consisted of none other than the incomparable Pastor Donnie Mclurkin, Tejan Edwards, Micah Stampley, and the house choir which was led by the angelic sound of Missy Destiny James, under the direction of yours truly.

My transition from Long Island to Brooklyn made such a difference; I was now at the church for extensive hours on some days when necessary as my expectation as the head of the music ministry meant that I had to be dedicated one hundred percent. Minister Alistair had requested a transfer and was granted his desire. The choir was functioning at a spiritual high like never before; the gifts upon the young people was phenomenal as they were all uniquely blessed in their own way proliferating the glory of God. Missy Destiny was now the newest artist of McClurkin House. This young lady had proven herself to be a committed woman to the call of God. The friendship between us had blossomed from a rosebud to an award winning rose; I was totally confident that our friendship had nowhere to go than up. I was blessed that I could confide in her, which led me to share my spiritual encounter that the Lord had revealed concerning His people and how He was waiting for His people to get back to the heart of worship; He was waiting for the Saints to be committed to the ultimate goal, which was to proclaim the name of Jesus as God and Lord.

Today was a beautiful day; one could jokingly express that the sun was in a good mood. The horizon was stupendous and I knew that the Lord was happy to see the remnant pursuing His glory and it was manifesting in the beautiful days that we were experiencing. I sat around my keyboard lifting up songs of worship to the risen King while enjoying the vivacious view of nature. Mrs. Fraser was pleasantly watering the flowers budding in her flowerbed while she worshipped with the melodious sounds resounding from my bedroom. The sound of the ringing telephone caught both our attention but she quickly reached into her pocket and retrieved the device and proceeded to answer. "Praise the Lord" she greeted the caller, I could hear her enthusiastic voice from where I sat and from the joy in her voice I knew she was ecstatic to hear the voice of the person on the other end of the line. "Sis Anna is that you, how are you?" From what I gather the caller was crying as her voice was cracking with every word. "Hold on Anna" Mrs. Fraser instructed as she placed the call on speaker in an effort to understand what she was saying. "It is me" Ma Anna confirmed, "is David home? I can't seem to get a hold of him on his mobile phone". I rushed from my bedroom and was now standing in the garden. Mrs. Fraser continued the call and replied "yes he's home, are you ok my beloved?" she asked the caller. "Yes I'm doing ok considering the circumstance"; "hold on Anna" she said, "here is David". "David" she greeted, her voice echoing through the speaker phone, "yes Ma I'm here what's going on?" "Son" she continued "it's your father; he has just been rushed to the hospital". I was stunned as she told me the disturbing details of how my dad had suffered a minor stroke and assured me that God was in control. I hung up after she informed me of the hospital where he was taken. I handed the phone to the woman of God who endeavored to console me and offered to drive me over to the Hospital. I had a heart rending instinct that my presence was needed; we quickly prepared ourselves and began the journey from Brooklyn to Long Island.

The traffic was unusually clear and allowed them to get there in record time. They parked in the parking lot of the enormous building and headed to the main floor and began to make inquiry; they were directed to the third floor of the Intensive Care Unit where he was admitted. David walked to the desk and introduced himself in an effort to receive vital information concerning his dad. The lovely nurse manager, Sedaine Lyn told him to hold on a few minutes while she checked the computer. She had a very warm smile and while typing, told David that all will be well as she knows the pain he was currently feeling. He was approached by the attending physician who assured him that his dad was stable and the worst was behind him. David was later told that he could visit him briefly as he needed total rest for the next couple of hours. David walked over to the waiting area and told Mrs. Fraser what the doctor told him. He tried to make himself as comfortable as possible while he waited for further instructions from the nurse. He was pacing the hall when he met his brothers who were returning from their brief visit. He was totally comfortable despite the awkwardness of his siblings, and greeted each of them with the Lord's blessings. It was now exactly ten minutes since he'd been waiting for the nurse when he was approached by his eldest brother who was a bit delayed and lagged behind the others. He explained to David that his dad was requesting to see him; he signaled to Mrs. Fraser that he would be right back. He trailed his brother and was led to a private room where his dad was hooked up to a heart monitor and tubes but was resting comfortably.

I began to wipe the tears that were like hot sauce in my eyes and walked over to him; I was surprised as my dad opened his eyes and spoke in a blurred tone "my son". The words touched the core of my heart and I was as the deserted little boy who would cry myself to sleep in wait for those exact words. I bent over towards him and made a heartfelt decision that I would forget the things that were behind and look towards the mark of the high calling. I began to direct my prayers to the Lord Jesus Christ in whom my confidence lied and interceded for a complete and swift recovery for my father. I was taken aback as he opened his eyes and held on to me tightly with his functioning hand. I smiled at him but continued to pray in audibility expecting a miraculous deliverance. I closed out the prayer and placed my lips to his ear and whispered "daddy your son is here". The nurse returned and informed us that the doctors' order was for him to get as much uninterrupted rest as possible. I kissed him carefully on his forehead and exited the room. The waiting room was now filled with many more familiar faces; Elder Mike had now joined his wife, along with Elder and Evangelist Johnson, Kylee, Daniel and Destiny. David was truly overwhelmed by those who had made the choice to be with him in his time of need; they each took a moment to encourage him and reassured him that it was well. David told them he had to conclude the visit as it was the doctor's order that his dad needed all the rest he could get in this critical moment. We held hands in unity and oneness of heart and prayed one last prayer of agreement and gave thanks unto the Lord for His grace and mercy.

David's began to spend most of his days at the hospital as he had made a commitment to spend quality time with his dad. Mr. Manner was rapidly recovering as expected; all glory and honor to Jehovah Rapha the healer who was his portion in his time of need. This unfortunate incident had allowed them to spend a lot of alone time and what the enemy meant for bad had now turned around for good; they had developed an unusual bond that was beyond belief. David had used every given moment to minister the gospel of peace to his father and his father accepted Jesus as his personal Savior, making the vow to commit his life and receive water baptism. It was exactly one week and his father was discharged from the hospital with total capability; his physical and mental members were all intact.

The revival was approaching speedily and everyone was giving unselfishly of themselves to meet the requirements for the meeting. David was giving a hundred and ten percent to the choir and his dedication to the work of God was admired by Apostle Edwards and Elder Mike as they were in agreement that this was a chosen young man sent to them by God. Elder Mike had openly expressed his gratitude to David for holding down the fort even after the decision that Minister Alistair had made concerning his departure. David knew that he would have to be a man of his word as a wise man once said 'anointing without character is folly'. He was present at each rehearsal and God was there to keep him standing as the man that he was called to be. He was an exceptional leader and was also becoming a fast mentor to the youth and even to those who were considered his elders. Of course there were times when it seems like it was a bit overwhelming but he was ready to do whatever it took to cross his Jordon.

David kept God at the center of his being and in so doing he realized that even when life was not going according to plan, his motive had to remain the same to execute the will of God. The enemy would always come to derail you but one thing that was clear in David's mind was that he was determined not to let the enemy triumph over his purpose. The enemy only comes to kill, steal, and destroy but the Lord came that we might have life and have it more abundantly. The days had gone by so quickly it was only one week before the revival. He had held on to the word of the Lord and everything was at the peak of musical excellence. David entertained the thought 'I have acquired what is, because one should not be only a hearer of the word but a doer also'. He believed in the word and was delighted in it because he knew that the word of God was quick and powerful and sharper than any two edged sword. He knew that the grass would be greener on the other side and as the words of the song declared 'by and by when the morning comes, when all the saints of God are gathered home, we'll tell the story of how we overcome and we'll understand it better by and by'.

The sun had risen like the morning glory. David opened the door of his bedroom and made his way outside the house; there was a peace that was pulling him into the presence of God. He knew he had to submit to the Holy Spirit. He walked across the grass and felt the mist of the fluffy like cushion massaging his feet as he took the short walk going as he was led. David stopped at the designated spot and there he lifted his eyes towards the heavens and was comforted in his heart that he was where the Lord wanted him at this present time. He closed his eyes and opened his heart to hear what the Lord wanted to say to him; he knew that the power of God would usher him into the realm of the Spirit. He sat in awe as he waited for the still soft voice that was always a whisper away and in mid thought the anointing moved upon him in a powerful way that he had to surrender, falling to his knees. He whispered the word of submission and spoke "speak Lord thine servant heareth", and in that instance he heard a voice ministering to his soul saying "son it is well, always know that I'm only a prayer away". The tears began to flow like a rushing river and from that moment life became a little bit clearer. David understood that the love of God was proven to keep him through any obstacle; he began to smile at the wonder of the Sovereign King. He remained in total solace and held on to the hope that God had everything under control. The sound of footsteps approaching made him aware of his surroundings; he opened his eyes, and standing in close proximity was none other than Elder Mike, the man who was a mentor and a father to him. Mike stood speechless and in that moment he quietly gave glory to the Lord for allowing him to be a part of the life of such an amazing human being. He then came to the conclusion that David was truly a man after God's own heart; he smiled at his son and they remained in silence in reverence to the will of God.

The appointed day finally arrived; today was the beginning of three full days of power and manifestation in the anointing. The Sanctuary was filled in every aspect of the word and Mother Williams was making sure that everything was in check as she flashed her intoxicating smile to every person. I sat at the keyboard and waited as the praise team made their way to the pulpit. Sis Destiny took her position followed by Abigail and Hannah and the women began to worship the Lord in the fullness of power and in a few minutes the glory of the Lord hovered over the house. They lifted their voices and invoked the presence of God while inviting the congregation to feel free to join them in total praise unto the Lord. We were now charged in the anointing and the ladies left the pulpit as Apostle and Evangelist Edwards took over and officially declared "this revival is now in the hand of God". Evangelist Kylee was introduced as the night's moderator; she was splendidly attired from her head to her feet. Kylee had always been known to be a trendsetter to young ladies whether they were of the faith or otherwise. Kylee entered the pulpit and began to magnify the Lord; she was already saturated in the Holy Spirit as the praise and worship team had reached a level of excellence and it felt as if the portals were opened over us. The woman of God continued to worship as the tears ran down her cheeks; she understood the move of the Spirit and was well aware that it was time to call the guest Psalmist to the pulpit. "Church" she spoke in a broken voice "at this time without further ado, please stand and give the Lord a shout of praise as we welcome the anointed messenger of God, none other than Pastor Donnie McClurkin as he comes to take us into the throne room of God". We stood in reverence to the Lord as the man of God entered the podium and rang with a thunderous sound "behold he come riding on the cloud, shining like the sun as the trumpet roll, lift your voice it's the year of Jubilee and out of Zion's hill salvation comes". The church went into a total uproar as he lifted his voice in total worship; we began to lift our voice as he had directed us to join him in worshipping Jesus our Lord. The man of God kept us fixated on the one true and living God as he led us in worship one song after another. The house was in liberation and I knew that the Lord was hovering over us; I was now on my knees with my had lifted in total surrender, giving Jesus what was due to Him as the theologian declared 'Christ died for us so we could live for him'. I was committed in every way to be a doer of the word in Romans 12:1-2, knowing that it was the least we could do after all He had sacrificed for us.

Pastor Donnie left the pulpit and Evangelist Kylee stood before us once again, this time she was shouting praise to the Sovereign God. The congregation was in one accord in worship as the mothers were ministering to the broken. The service was now in the hand of the Lord and we knew according to the scripture in 1 Thessalonians 5:19 that the word declares 'Quench not the Spirit', and with that revelation being surfaced, the Lord was in total control. The Speaker took his position and waited with heartfelt joy as the anointing moved upon the people allowing his job to be less complicated. Bishop Brown was no stranger to us as he had made the journey once again from London, England to bring fort what thus sayeth the Lord. The topic for the weekend was "Follow me and I will make you fishers of men." This was birthed directly after last year's revival in Apostle Edwards and it was truly a word for all who was ready to die daily. Bishop Brown began to slowly move in excellence as the Spirit led him, going directly into the scripture Matthew 4:19, "as Jesus walked by the sea of Galilee seeing two brothers casting their nets into the sea for they were fishermen. The first being Simon Peter the other his brother Andrew and he spoke unto them saying: follow me and I will make you fishers of men". Bishop began to break bread with us and we ate the food of the Spirit that was prepared for us. As it is written in the Holy Scriptures that 'men should not live by bread alone but instead we should live by every word that comes from the mouth of

God'. The power of God was upon the Bishop and as he gave the word, many were delivered and even more so, hundreds decided to give their lives to the Lord.

The weekend continued in the same anointing. We were now in day two of our revival and the Sanctuary was charged with worship; the choir had opened the service with radical worship and Sister Destiny was in a comfortable flow as she took the choir to the inner court, allowing the congregation to enter into His presence. They closed out their worship session and allowed the young Tejan Edwards to lead us into the holies of holies. This young man had such a transparency about him that was so significant to the believers and unbelievers alike. He knew that the secret to get to the heart of anyone was to be a servant who was obedient to the call of God, and that was a proven factor which allowed him to minister in another dimension of worship. The pace was set as the two speakers took their positions: the first was our own newly installed Elder Onajhe Morgan who spoke the undiluted word of God from a perspective to reach the lost while encouraging them that it only took a change of heart to become a soldier in the army of the Lord. He totally brought us to a place of spiritual wisdom to reach the lost in our generation. He left the pulpit and the final speaker for the night graced the podium in the person of Pastor Charles Williams; his accolades were previously read in our hearing. This was a man of God that lived a life that modeled Christ in every sense of the word; he was the newly installed Pastor of Purpose Life Church which was changing the face of a nation one soul at a time. He dove into the word with the same topic, but it was customary for him to use visual aids to bring his much needed points across. He opened by asking the congregation to stand and get our minds focused on where the Lord was taking us. He began to pray and asked the Lord to have His way and also to bless the previous speaker, young Elder Morgan who did an awesome job. He continued by introducing his sub topic 'There is glory in your story". Pastor Williams reminded us that Simon Peter had toiled all night and had caught nothing until he was directed by Jesus; he tied the scriptures and words together. He initially taught us that in order to get to the heart of the matter; one must be interested in another's misfortune and short comings. Simon had been transformed from a rowdy fisherman evolving into one of Jesus' apostle who on the day of Pentecost preached with boldness adding about three thousand souls to the Kingdom. He took the church to a place of mirroring the Savior for the God that He was; not as the religious God that was angry all the time but as the compassionate God who ministered to all our needs. He came in the flesh so he could relate to every feeling of our infirmities. This word had come home to me even in the person of Elder Michael Fraser who without reservation not only invited me to my first revival but invited me into his home and ultimately into his family. I was touched by the ministry of this humble servant of God and was deep in thoughts and was startled as I heard him call my name inviting me to minister in the final moments as he made the invitation for those who had never had the opportunity to give their lives to the Lord Jesus. I made my way to the pulpit and he laid his hands upon me and whispered in my ear, "son you are a trusted servant of the Lord; keep the faith and toil for the cause of salvation". He walked back to his seat and with an overwhelmed heart I ministered to the Lord with a new mindset; the altar was filled and this turned out to be a revival indeed.

"Michael" Mrs. Fraser called from the family room "let's go, and where's David? Girls come on let go" she announced frantically, "remember the final day is always the most challenging and we have to get there an hour early as was advised by Evangelist Edwards so we can get into consecration before the start of the service. "Ok Petrina" he responded "I'm just getting my bible". We got to the church and before we could exit the vehicle I was met by Evangelist Kylee who informed me that that I should brace myself for what she had to share. "David" she spoke in a formal tone "you have a special visitor", I looked at her with curiosity hoping for the impossible because as far as I was concerned, it could be anyone at this point. She smiled and broke the silence and assured me by saying "boy don't get your head all in a frenzy; your dad is here and he is waiting for you in the foyer". He braced himself and walked in a new felt confidence to the building; he had a new sense of joy that melted his heart 'my father is here'. Mother Williams stood in the foyer holding a tray with a glass of water tending to the need of the visitor who had introduced himself as Mr. Manner. David began to triple his steps and waited for his father to finish the water; he greeted his dad with loving embrace, with gratitude, and appreciation of the healing power of Jesus Christ. He was standing tall looking his normal self as the once confident and self-assured man he had grown to appreciate. He was assured by Mother Williams that his father was in capable hands and he hugged him again with the promise of seeing him before the service began.

The revival was headed for greatness; David could feel the breaking of chains and strongholds as the team prayed and prepared the house for the invocation of the Holy Ghost. The choir had once again performed at the highest level of their gift; this proved that every sacrificial moment spent in rehearsal was well worth it and truly paid off. My heart was joyous as I served in leading the group of talented and anointed young people. I thanked God for His goodness toward me; one who was crying in Lodi bar but who knew that time spent in God was never time lost. We surrendered our will wholeheartedly to the Lord and was joined by Psalmist Micah Stampley, who was the guest minister for the final day of the feast. He lifted his voice and led us in one of his latest single 'our God is greater'; the power of God swept the house to a new high and the entire congregation was blessed with his powerful voice. Micah was known to those who followed his ministry as a humble man of God who dedicated his life to worship the Lord in spirit and truth. There was a sweet spirit in the Sanctuary as we gave the Lord the glory that was due to Him. I looked in the congregation and saw my father lifting his hands to the Lord in worship and I knew that God was doing a mighty work in him. The worship was so amazing and now I really understood why the Lord inhabited the praises of His people; the people were crying before the Lord and worshipping the Lord withholding nothing.

Apostle Edwards made his way to the pulpit and began to thank God for allowing us to be under an open heaven. He encouraged the congregation as we quietly ministered the final song titled 'brokenness is what I long for'; with the psalmist allowing the Holy Spirit to saturate every person that was in the room. "Saints of God" Pastor Edwards addressed the church "Jesus is not here, He is in us and around us, and something good is about to happen". He looked at the flock and all those who had made their way to be among us in spite of, and declared in a prophetic voice "tell your neighbor something good is about to happen". "Come on beloved, give God praise for the powerful ministry of the choir and put something on it for the Psalmist, our friend and bother Micah Stampley". The musician went into a moment of uplifted interlude and with each instrument in one accord; we were led to a praise break session. The isles were filled with both young and old and even the toddlers began to dance like David danced as the scripture declared. We were having a glorious time before the Lord and I knew that the Lord was well pleased. Apostle continued to speak with thanksgiving in his voice, "brothers and sisters, God has truly been generous to us and I'm here to tell you that it's about to overflow in this hour. Please keep standing as it's time for the word; yes beloved the Lord has a word for us tonight. He blessed us on Friday, he blessed us on Saturday, and He is about to bless us again. Now somebody help me declare that now He's gonna give the icing on the cake, let me hear you shout 'Sunday'". We all shouted "Sunday" and he responded "bless us Lord". The praises went to another height once more as the worshippers gave the Lord one last shout.

Apostle stood and began to wipe the excess perspiration in the second handkerchief that was provided by his armor bearer, none other than my mentor and father figure Elder Mike. He stood back and took a brief pause then began to introduce the speaker. He lifted his voice and read the well-deserved accolade of none other than Bishop T D Jakes, the one who was selected to be the voice in this final moment. Bishop Jakes made his way to the podium and went into the same mode of worship which led to another praise break. He stood and looked to the heavens in amazement at the outpour of worship that flooded the room. I took my eyes from the speaker for a moment and focused my attention in the direction where my father had been seated; I was a little concerned as I realized that spot was now vacant. I was immediately comforted when I saw him standing in all his masculinity exalting Jesus with the assistance of the woman of God, Mother Williams by his side. I exhaled and focused my attention back to the speaker who was already starting the much anticipated message.

"Saints of the most high God" Bishop Jakes spoke in his usual effective tone "I am going to take a slightly different route" he chuckled and continued "don't worry I am going to take you to your final destination". "Ok" he continued "that went over some of your heads but be assured I'll take you back to the theme for the weekend, Amen", he shouted ;"amen" we chorused in total confidence knowing that if anyone could bring this ship to dock it was this man of God. "People of God I'll be subtitling my message 'if you want to change your world you have to change your mind'; they work hand in hand". The congregation began to lift praises again to the Lord as he repeated the words. "My dear brothers and sisters, let me assure you" he continued in a thunderous tone "if you don't change your mind you will never affect change". The Lord told his disciples in the book of Acts 1:8, "But ye shall receive power, after that the Holy Ghost is come upon you, and ye shall be witnesses unto me both in Jerusalem, and in all Judaea, and in Samaria and unto the uttermost part of the earth". "Now this scripture came to my mind because Jesus was God in the flesh and if anyone knew what it would take for effectual witnessing, it would be Him. He was directing this charge to Peter the curser, the denier, the all-time ruffian, and also to doubtful Thomas who was dumb as a doorpost. I often wondered how could he after seeing all that this Man had done, even being present while He performed innumerable miracles; seriously, how could this brother still remain doubtful? The mere fact that he commanded an unfruitful tree to be dried from the root and it had to obey. I often reasoned with myself and always came to the same conclusion that only God could display the patience that Jesus exercised to some of the characters that walked with him. I don't know about them but I would be secretly interceding and giving thanks that God who knew me as messed up as I am or let me rephrase that as messed up as we are and still He died while we were yet sinners. Now I want you to shout hallelujah if you agree with me that it must have been a big God who would chose you and me to go into all the world and preach the good news". "Now beloved of God" he continued "I only say this to bring you to a place that we can all become witnesses of the Lord by telling self, 'tonight I am taking back the wheel to this here ride, I will not allow you to minister to my mind, it is time for change' and watch the change that will come". He preached the uncompromised word of God and brought it home to the rich, poor, the skinny, the not so skinny, and all who were blessed to be under the sound of his voice. The altar call was made as the Psalmist Micah Stampley song the popular song "worthy is the lamb". Bishop Jakes invited all the speakers for the weekend along with the minister to join him at the altar. Apostle Edwards was then handed the mike and he invited everyone who was ready for change to take a step of faith. "I don't know what your most urgent situation is or what is currently blocking you from being an effective disciple, but the Holy Ghost is here to meet you and as He did in Acts chapter 1 so will He lead you in His will".

The altar was flooded to capacity and we hurried to receive from the Lord. My father was a part of the number of us who made our way to meet our destiny. My heart was truly blessed as he stood beside me; I held out my hand as we waited in anticipation for what was to come. The service was then handed over into the competent hand of Bishop Brown who began to move in the prophetic. He prophesied as the spirit led and ministered to the individual needs of those who stood before him. The man of God was working in the realm of the spirit and was led by the Spirit to my father; he began to minister to him and my dad became transparent before the Lord with much fear and trembling. We were now joined by Elder Fraser who through discernment, knew that my dad needed all the moral support he could receive and he was willing to serve as he was led. Bishop Brown was moved by compassion and began to fervently pray for my father as the spirit gave him utterance. He was just a few moments into the prayer and Jesus worked a supernatural miracle where my dad was immediately set free both in mind and body. David watched as his father's countenance changed and he knew there and then that 'it was finished'.

CHAPTER 11

My life was going as anticipated as prophecy was being fulfilled. There was a vast increase being poured upon me especially in the recording industry. From the outside looking in, one would describe me as the ultimate picture of success. My album as we speak was recently nominated for a coveted Stellar award in four categories which confirmed that God was working on my behalf; I was nominated new artist of the year, artist of the year, male vocalist of the year, and CD of the year. My first single had topped the charts consecutively for a number of weeks, and was recently dropped to the number two position after being replaced by the duet with myself and Destiny from the album titled "living life on purpose". I was the new prince of gospel and I was reminded of that wherever I went; truly this had become bigger than I'd ever imagine. My life had taken off as a whirlwind and I began to have reservations in many aspects associated with serving the Lord in the publics' eyes. There were so many questions that had begun to plague my thoughts but above them all, the fear of failing God had taken center stage in my mind. I sat facing the wall in my secluded bedroom and wondered 'had I became one of the many that had been overtaken by the cares of life and had forsaken my first love'. I sat at the edge of my oversized bed and realized that I had made such a gigantic transition moving from my childhood home. It was a humble abode despite the living circumstances; it was a fact that my life was spiritually inclined because of the unique relationship I developed with the Lord while I was there. I tried in every way to close out the thoughts that had become a thorn in my flesh. I made my way to the lavished ensuite and began to prepare myself for the day ahead. I was previously advised by Elder Michael that it was time that I took the initiative and apply for a driver's license; I took the test and that was successfully accomplished. I recently received my New York State driver's license and was on my way to purchase my very own car.

I stepped out of the shower and attired myself allowing my outer appearance to mask the inner battles which had now become a part of me and it had proven to be successful. I sat in a daze as I admired the flowers that were blooming beautifully in the garden and confirmed in my spirit that

Mrs. Fraser truly had a green thumb; she was gifted and brought out the best in these little plants that she tended to. The magnolias had sprung up to be as beautiful as the name and had become a sight for the eyes to behold. I was deeply lost in thoughts just admiring the flowers and reflecting on the fact that we were even compared to these beauties in the word of God. My meditation was abruptly interrupted by the familiar sound of a vehicle, one I knew all too well. Sis Kylee was right on schedule which didn't come as a surprise to me in any shape or form. My big sis had acquired the nick name AOT 'always on time' by the youth department because of her natural ability to always be punctual. Kylee made her final approach into the driveway, opened the door of her parents Range Rover and walked towards the door with Daniel right behind her; this had been a second home to her and Daniel for most of their childhood. They rang the doorbell and I could hear her voice from my bedroom as she made a declaration of her arrival; Daniel remained less audible and smiled as he admired his sister's enthusiasm and spunk.

Mrs. Fraser opened the door and greeted her God children who were just like her own. I could hear the sound of laughter as it echoed throughout the house and I was suddenly reminded of the joy that was associated with this home. I could smell the sweet aroma of cocoa and fresh baked croissants being prepared and decided that that was my cue to make my appearance. Daniel's voice became ecstatic as he heard the footsteps approaching, "bro is that you"? he inquired; I took a few more steps and responded to my big brother in an equally vibrant tone, "yes bro it is thine humble side-kick". Daniel began to chuckle as he often did when I responded in that way. I got to the kitchen and kissed Mrs. Fraser on the cheek and greeted the guys as I joined them at the dining table. We began to converse as we discussed the events of the Kingdom and how the Lord was doing a mighty work in the nation. We finished our food, cleaned up, and bid farewell to their house mother and exited the home focusing our main objective. Kylee and Daniel had volunteered to accompany me to the car dealership to purchase my very first vehicle.

We arrived at the dealership and Kylee handed the key to the valet as we continued on a short trip to the showroom. My heart was in deliberation as to which model of vehicle I would chose; my final choice was between an Audi A7 and an Infinity but whichever of the two would be a win-win in my perspective. They entered the door of the showroom and was greeted by the stunning woman of God, Sister Paulette who was a member of the congregation and also Sister Destiny's Godmother; she was affectionately known to us young people as Aunty P. She greeted each of us individually making us feel loved with her authentic way of ensuring each person in her company felt special. "I've been sitting on the edge of my seat awaiting for my guest of honor to arrive; so David are you ready to take the big plunge?" she beamed flashing her coveted signature smile that was known to warm even the darkest room. "Amen" David responded and smiled at the jovial woman who stood barely five feet tall which made him feel like a giant. I was quickly brought back to reality and felt slightly double mined in the effort to go all the way; I'd never thought that I would be driving my own car at this stage of my life but purchasing one was on my own terms. We walked over to the area where the luxury vehicles were displayed and I understood what Aunty Paulette meant when she informed me 'you will get whatever your heart desires'. She proudly said "we have kept the reputation of delivering in the highest magnitude of excellence". David knew that Jehovah Jireh had made provisions for him to be in this juncture at this time in his life and with that brief thought they followed the woman of God as she led them to the beautifully waxed and gleaming machines.

Daniel's eyes began to spark as the he came face to face with all the floor displays. He looked me in the eyes and spoke in a fatherly tone "ok mister what's it gonna be?" Everything was going in a frenzy as there were so many cars to choose from, but I was convinced that the Lord would make the final decision. Aunty P interrupted the awkward moment and told us to wait while she got the salesman who would help us in the first stage of the purchase. As we waited, Kylee broke the silence and held my hands in an effort to reduce the anxiety among us; I smiled at her implying 'I'm ok' but she held me even firmer. "I'm back my darlings", the spunky woman announced! "And look who decided to join us?" We all began to smile to see Demoy, Aunty Paulette's youngest son who appeared with an equally jovial look on his face. He was professionally attired and looked the part of an experienced salesman that made me even more confident than ever to be in the capable hands of a friend and brother. Demoy began to educate us on the different models of vehicles, and in what felt like only a few minutes, he had successfully managed to give us the best views and reviews of the machines that were most safe and reliable. I entered the vehicles one model after the other and began to examine the features and comfort; I was finally at my final decision concerning what I needed and was hoping that my friends would be in agreement. Everyone's attention was now focused on me as they eagerly awaited my decision. I looked at my audience and decided that a little suspense was necessary at times. Daniel chucked and teased "ok bro you can let us exhale now, what's it going to be?" I nodded and responded in a calm tone "yeah bro you can breathe now", I walked over to the car of my choice and laid my hand on the roof, "amen" Kylee shouted excitedly as I opened the door of the immaculate white Audi A7 and sat in the plush comfort of the fully loaded vehicle. The approval was made from all my supporters as they congratulated me with hugs and kisses. Aunty Paulette embraced me and waited as I exited the car and led me to the office to finalize the purchase.

We drove up to the house and as was expected I had an audience. Elder Mike walked towards the vehicle and held out his arms and hugged me as he expressed his approval of my excellent choice. I smiled and handed him the keys as he continued to examine the cutting edge machine. I walked to my bedroom and closed the door behind me and began the mask the hurt that had been brewing in my inner being; the mental war that developed in my mind was becoming unbearable. I shrugged my shoulders, trying with every effort to relinquish my pain. I walked to the bathroom and began to wash the tears from my eyes but after a few moments I realized that my sorrow wasn't going to be washed away physically. The knock on my bedroom door was intense; I made every effort to relax as I answered "come in". Kylee entered the room and closed the door with a turn of the lock; she looked me in the eyes with a look of concern and eventually she broke the silence and spoke with a heart of concern. "Are you ok little brother?" she questioned me in her usual motherly tone; I looked at her making every effort to hide the pain that had kept me in bondage and smiled my usual smile and assured her as best as I could my repeating my famous words "it is well". Kylee tightened her grip and looked at me with tear filled eyes and replied "yes it is, for the Lord who has ordained you is able to sustain you". She released my arm and took a seat at the edge of the bed and waited. I paused and deliberated whether or not I wanted to disclose what was truly bothering me. I broke the silence and began to express all that contributed to this state of oppression; I explained all that had kept me in an overwhelmed state of mind. The tears were now pouring from my eyes uncontrollably and at that moment I knew that the Lord was releasing me from the demon that was trying to keep my mind in captivity. We spoke for approximately an hour as Kyle listened intently to everything thing without interruption.

"David" Kylee spoke and began to console me as best as she could, "I'm here for you, I know that things are moving like a whirlwind. I know that change can be overwhelming at times but despite what's going on at this present moment, be encouraged. The scripture declares that, weeping may endure for a night but joy comes in the morning". I smiled at her and held my composure as she ministered to me. I gave God praise for allowing me to cross path with such a sympathetic human being who had proven herself as a true woman of God. I excused myself and went to the bathroom and quickly splash my face with water from the faucet in an effort to rejoin everyone, who from the sound of laughter had now made their way to the kitchen. "You ready to join the gang?" she questioned as I returned to the room "amen" I replied holding my head high. Kylee's smile broke as she looked me in the eye "hey kiddo everything's is going to be ok", she then reached into her purse and placed a business card in my hand. I took the card and immediately recognize the familiar face. "David I need you to make a call to this man of God," the image on the card was that of Pastor Charles Williams of Purpose Life Church. This minister was a highly esteemed member of the Kingdom and praised for his genuine relationship with the younger generation. "David" Kylee continued "there is nothing too hard for God except when we choose not to hand it over". "I will give Pastor Charles a call to give him a heads up that he'll be hearing from you. I shook my head as she continued to speak, "I know that you are a little scared and even hesitant right now but I'm confident that after you've met with this man, your outlook on life will change; he is just awesome"

Elder mike was holding the keys to my car with a smile on his face; "here you go son" he said as he dangled the shiny object in the air. I returned the smile and took the keys placing it in my pocket and walked over to join Daniel in the family room where his attention was focused on the TV as he watched the sports highlights on ESPN. "Hi brother, is everything ok?" he hit pause on the remote in the middle of a basketball highlight, "yes" I answered with a little more confidence knowing that with God all things were possible. Mrs. Fraser who was busy in the kitchen from the time of our arrival called from the dining room and announced "dinner is served". We all took our desired seats with great anticipation knowing that this meal was as delectable as the aroma and was expected to satisfy our taste buds. The girls where already at the table and were deeply engaged in a conversation about my new addition as they each complimented me on my choice. I thanked them for the compliments as Abbigail continued to speak of the beauty and uniqueness of the vehicle. We sat in silence as Elder Mike blessed the food and thanked the Lord for His blessing on my life. The meal was being served and as was expected it very delicious totally satisfying all my cravings and desires.

We remained at the table as Mrs. Fraser supplied us with a mouth-watering dessert which to my surprise was a beautiful customized cake in the shape of a car with a picture of me on it. I looked at her and shook my head saying "I should've known, you guys are so amazing" I smiled, "just amazing". She placed the cake before me and began to speak, "no son the spotlight is on you, you are amazing and we just want you to know that the Lord is mighty proud of you. Now go ahead cut the first slice as we are anxious to dig in this dessert that promises to make our day a little sweeter", "amen" I agreed and placed the knife taking a slice removing the door. "Hmm" the words uttered from my soul "this was the most delicious cake I'd ever tasted", Mrs. Fraser smiled and added "that's the reaction you'll get when you take a bite of the pastries from 'Mala and Majie's Delectables'. I took another slice before passing it around and watched the cake slowly disappear before my eyes. The sun began to set so Kylee and Daniel gathered their belonging and prepared themselves to depart; they bid everyone farewell and left the room. I remove the partially full garbage and headed behind them as they made their way to the door. I quickly placed the bag in its rightful place and hurried back to see them off. Kylee was waiting outside the vehicle and hugged me again and smiled as she spoke to me, "it was a good day, now be safe and enjoy your blessing, see you soon". I walked to the driver's seat where Daniel was waiting patiently for his sister and thanked him for being a supporter and friend. He hugged me and returned the same words to me.

I thanked Mrs. Fraser for the meal and the surprise and made my way to my room making sure to close the door behind me. I walked over to the dresser and picked up the card and placed it in my wallet before heading to the shower. I finished my bath, got dressed and made my way outside to get a little more familiar with my brand new car. I opened the door and was astonished to see Elder Mike laying hands as he blessed the vehicle using anointing oil; I continued toward the vehicle and he turned in my direction and gestured for me to join him. I did as was told and began to agree as he prayed fervently for my safety and guidance as I go on my daily endeavors; then we closed out the prayer giving God thanks once more. I opened the driver side door and the man of God walked to the opposite side of the car and sat in the passenger's seat; he exhaled and looked me in the eyes and asked the popular question of the day "are you ok?" I looked away and began to tell him of all that was bombarding me even to this point. He was attentive as I spoke and unloaded my heart explaining that Kylee had furnished me with the business card for Pastor Williams and made me promise to follow up on the opportunity. He was in total agreement and encouraged me to make the appointment as quickly as possible, with the assurance of the good report that Pastor Williams had with his direct and sincere approach to serving in the Kingdom.

We began to examine the car and agreed it was even bigger on the inside and offered all the luxury that was expected for the value. We made our way to the house and retired to our separate sections. I was awakened by my phone as it rang continually; I retrieved it and quickly answered before losing the caller again. "Praise the Lord" I greeted "praise the Lord my brother" Kylee greeted, "I'm sorry to wake you", "amen" I responded "it's ok, I was between prayers but time is far spent". "Well I just wanted to give you a heads up on what we spoke about yesterday", "amen" I stated "go ahead". "I spoke to Pastor Williams and he's awaiting your call; don't worry you're in good hands so do what you have to and believe that the Lord has already given him the tools to bless you". We spoke for a few brief moments and ended the call with me promising to call the man of God as soon as possible. I placed the phone on the charger and dove into my morning routine seeking the Lord in prayer and worship. I had previously committed my day for fasting and intersession. The clock struck three o' clock and I got up from the floor and entered the ensuite and prepared for the day. I released my phone from the charger and dialed the number on the card; my heart began to beat at a faster pace as I waited for the man of God, Pastor Williams to answer. "Bless the Lord he greeted", "praise the Lord Sir" I responded "this is David". "Amen" he responded enthusiastically, "so good to hear from you" his voice was exactly as I'd remember from the youth revival; a heart that was sincere and full of compassion. We spoke briefly and Pastor Williams scheduled for me to meet him at his office the following day. I hung up the phone and exhaled at the hope that was evident before me.

I allowed the phone to ring for an unusually longer period giving Anna the extra time that she might need to get to it; she answered the call and was excited as always to hear my voice. We chatted for a while as I updated her about my recent purchase and all that was going on in my life. We were still on the phone as I entered the kitchen and poured out a cup of hot water and added a half of a lemon and sweetened it to taste. I was excited to be able to have this time with her as she had always been a motherly figure. I was really missing this part of my life and decided I really needed to make an extra effort to see her. I close the conversation with the promise of visiting her as soon as time permitted. We said our goodbyes and I smiled at the thought of her face as her excitement escalated when I informed her that I would see her very soon. I opened the refrigerator and began to customize a meal that I thought would keep my mind above waters; how was it possible I thought, to move from one extreme to the other in the blink of an eye. It was evident that I was living between two opinions in a catastrophic state of mind.

I woke up to the buzz of my alarm clock and immediately busied myself in an effort to get to my appointment on time. I went into the bathroom and set my face before the Lord singing songs of praise as I showered. I carefully dressed myself making sure I wasn't over or under dressed for the occasion. I must have changed at least three times in an effort to achieve the look I wanted; I smiled at myself in the mirror and thought 'well after all I need to look the part to line up even a tiny bit to the car that was sitting in the garage'. I closed my bedroom door and was surprised to hear Elder Mike's voice in the kitchen; quickening my steps I made my way to greet him before I left the house. He was engaged in a phone conversation but held his finer up to gesture he'd be off briefly. I poured myself a cup of hot tea and sat for a moment as he closed out the phone call. "Hi son" he greeted as I took a sip of the hot beverage; "you look rather dapper today, special occasion I perceive". I placed the cup on the center of the Island and reminded him that today was my appointment to meet with Pastor Williams. He apologized for not remembering and immediately asked for my permission to breathe a word of prayer. I bowed my head giving him the notion to go ahead; he began to lift up salutations to the Lord and cried out to God to have His perfect way. He closed out the prayer asking the Lord to take the wheel over my life today both physically and spiritually.

The temperature gage signified that the vehicle had reached its proper heating requirement to be driven. I slowly backed out of the driveway and began my journey to what I was calling 'destiny'. The navigation system advised me that my commute to the church's office would be approximately twenty five minutes. I removed the sunglasses from its case and placed it on my face, then I selected the gospel station on the satellite radio and began focusing my mind on Jesus. "Change is gonna come" by Sharee Williams was the song playing and it motivated me to know that this was destiny and my change had truly come. I pulled into the parking lot of the massive property that housed the immaculate building with the sign that stated 'Purpose Life Church' and beneath that was written 'Where everyone had purpose'. I carefully parked my car in the visitors section and slowly made my way from the vehicle. I was finally here; my knees began to buckle and my mouth was instantly loosing moisture. I began to encourage myself giving the Lord thanks for allowing me the privilege of journeying mercies. I made my way towards the beautifully structured multi-story building and began to admire the architecture, scrutinizing every detail of the facility. The beautiful glass and marble features gave the building an inviting look that made it impossible for you not to admire as you go by. I pressed the locked button on my car key and made the final stretch to the entrance of the church.

The music was playing in sweet serenity as I entered the interior of the building. I was in tune to the great selection of worship that flowed in the atmosphere. My confidence began to boost as I walked briskly towards the glass like office; the infrastructucture was amazing and the beauty on the inside was intoxicating. My thoughts were suddenly interrupted with a loud greeting of a small figure that spoke in an enthusiastic voice "welcome to Purpose life Church, where everyone has purpose"." Hi how are you?" the petite woman called and prompted me to take a seat, "Pastor is expecting you", she continued "my name is Sister Chudey, I am Pastor Williams' secretary and this little person is my grandson Tohj". The little person of whom she spoke was the most handsome baby boy I'd ever seen in. I stretched out my hand and greeted her with a firm handshake as I stated "praise the Lord please to meet your acquaintance". "Hi Tohj" I continued speaking to the busy toddler as he made his way in my direction then hurried back to his grandmother. "You've met my daughter Tichina?" she began to make conversation in an effort to occupy time. I was immediately reminded of the woman of God of whom she spoke; how could I forget the sister who led the choir of this ministry. "Can I offer you anything while you wait? I have fresh coffee, tea or maybe a chilled bottle of water, whichever is your preference". I thanked her for the offer but assured her that I was ok at the moment. Sis Chudey busied herself at her desk and smiled while occasionally reminding me that it would be a brief wait. I picked up a copy of a magazine entitled 'Church World' and began to flip through the pages when I heard my name. I looked up and saw Pastor Charles standing at the office door and alongside him was his beautiful wife, First lady Williams. I stood and greeted the man and woman of God as they took turns hugging me. Pastor Williams instructed me to follow him and as we made our way to his office, Lady Williams remained in the office playing with baby Tohj.

I sat across from the man of God in his office noticing the crown molding on the celling. The oak desk was freshly polished which left a scent of orange lingering in the room. He looked across the table at me and smiled his genuine smile that made me remember why I'd agreed to be here. "Can I offer you a bottle of water" he asked still smiling; I thanked him and accepted the cold beverage. He stretched across the desk and held my hand, "let's open this session in prayer" he stated, "first things first". He finished the prayer and began to share the goodness of the Lord. I was now at a relaxed place and I knew the Lord had already begun the process of deliverance. He began to tell me about his family that was on the pictures on his desk to break the ice. We spoke briefly about his children then he stated "well that's enough about me; let's talk about what has brought you here today". I started to talk for a moment then decided that I'd backtrack, thinking to myself 'if I was going to do this why not do it right'. I began to open up as the man of God listened intently; I shared with him of my humble beginnings and how the Lord had called me from a child. I told him about the woman of God Ma Anna and how the Holy Ghost had used her to teach me about the presence of God. I spoke for and extensive time with tears in my eyes while I spoke of my father's property, and how the Lord had met with me so many times allowing the birthing of most of the music that I'd written. I then concluded with what had brought me to my present mental state of me believing that I'd left my first love and the guilt that plagued my thoughts.

Pastor Charles looked at me with a heart of sincerity and with uplifted hands he began to thank God for His mighty works and His wisdom in the situation before us. The man of God began to minister to my needs as he told me that the enemy has a way of deceiving even the very elect. "David" he spoke in a sincere tone "you have nothing to be guilty of, the scripture in the book of Third John chapter 1:2 states that the Lord himself spoke 'Beloved I wish above all things that you will prosper and be in good health, even as your soul prospers'. But there has been a device that has driven the church to derision in believing it's a sin to acquire blessings". He continued to state that it is written countless times in the word that the Lord had called us to prosperity. He reminded me that the bible declares 'it was the Lord that gives us power to get wealth', and we have no reason to be kept in captivity of mind for our achievements. "Son" he continued "I have been called some of the most evil names in the book, even by many of those in the Christian community for the blessing that has been bestowed on this ministry". He updated me on the hard work and commitment that it took for the church to reach its present state. They were the owner of one church in three locations, which facilitated campuses that housed schools from early childhood to post graduate Christian education. I listened with my whole heart as he became transparent before me; I began to feel the spirit of confusion being lifted from my mind and silently thanked the Lord. Pastor Williams looked me in the eyes and continued to speak "David, God has called you for a purpose and in this season the Lord is going to bless you abundantly in Jesus name. I have only one request and that is for you to go back to your father's house and go back to the place that you've met God and He'll close this chapter of your life". I obeyed the man of God and agreed to revisit the backside of the property.

I left the church with a much lifted spirit and made the journey back to my father's house; it was almost evening when I pulled into the driveway. Ma Anna was sitting outside as she awaited my arrival. She greeted me warmly with kisses and a loving embrace and watched as I made my way to the place of my spiritual birth. The place was exactly as I remembered and as I reached my designated spot I immediately felt the presence of the Lord overshadowing me. I closed my eyes and with a loud cry I began to worship God in His splendor as my heart was prone to give honor that was due to His name. The power of God brought me to my knees and I wept before the Lord surrendering my will and my way. I was now prostrate before the King and in this moment my clothes was not an important factor; all that I needed was right here, right now.

Chapter 12

Daniel, Elder Mike and I walked into the tuxedo shop; we had received the call that our suits were ready to be picked up. Mr. Howard James the owner of "J's Sharp Men's Tuxedo " located in the Purpose Life Mall was known for his expertise in authentically tailored men clothing. The sales personnel handed us our individual customized tuxedo and thanked us for making our choice J's. It was only two days away from the Stellar Awards and I was very excited for being nominated in four categories; that was truly above my expectations. God had blessed me beyond boundaries and I knew that my purpose was to lift up the name of Jesus and use my voice to the glory of God. I was quiet for the rest of the commute as I reflected on the journey of life. My thoughts went as far back to the very first day I entered the compound of my father's company. I walked into the facility with doubt and fear wondering how I got to this place; a life that seemed like hope had forgotten my name. I can remember the faces as if it was yesterday; each stare asked a different question but everyone's voice was silent. I was eventually taken to the lower level of the massive building and was placed under the supervision of Mr. Fraser. I had taken one glimpse of the soft spoken man and immediately I was comforted knowing that the hand of God was on him. It only took a few days for us to develop a bond as of a father to a son; it was then that I realized that hope was alive.

Elder Mike pulled onto the grounds where the award was scheduled to take place and parked the car. We made our way to the security desk and I provided the required pass. We were given the ok and we continued to the area that was designated for sound check. This was the first of two rehearsals that was required of me as I was blessed to be one of the performers at the event. Elder Mike and Daniel followed as the security led us to the stage area where the band was already in progress. Elder Mike broke the silence as the stranger left our company and began to encourage me saying he was confident that I was going to be excellent. I smiled and agreed with the man of God knowing that it was often spoken of me that I had an excellent spirit. Daniel was silent but gave me a look of assurance which meant he was in agreement with the statement. I made my way to the main stage and joined the band members and the scheduled performers. I was greeted with joy and laughter by everyone who was happy to finally make my acquaintance and the feeling was naturally mutual as I felt at home with them. The band went straightway into the intro for the song "Lord you're worthy"; I was brought back to the day that this song was birthed and with that reminder I gave everything I had. We went over the song a few times until the producer ended the session and praised the Lord for blessing me with the powerful and unique gift to pull in the anointing.

The drive from the venue was remarkable; both Mike and Daniel were uplifted in spirit and spoke in high pitched tones for the duration of the journey. Daniel was overjoyed at the excellence of God on my life and kept thanking the Lord for His grace and favor that was bestowed upon me. We got to his destination and I thanked my friend for his continuous support and for being a true brother. I knew that this was an orchestrated plan that the Lord had put in place over my life and suddenly my soul felt fulfilled. We continued the final journey looking back at what had gone through the door that had been opened unto me through the legendary Donnie. I continued and reminded the man of God that the journey had started even before that; I explained that it all began when the Lord brought me into his life. He kept his eyes on the road and began to explain to me all that the Lord had spoken to him when I was brought under his mentorship on the job. I was astounded to know that he and Mrs. Fraser had lost their son at only a few days old and the Lord had told him that I was brought to him as an answer to their heartfelt desire. I was sad to hear of his lost and uttered a silent prayer asking the Lord to never make me fail this family.

I continued with my routine the following morning when I woke up and made my way to the back of the house where I would seek the Lord. The morning air was cool and inviting as I stretched out in His presence and gave God what was due to Him. My heart was at one with His Spirit as I embarked on the journey that He'd called me to. I worshipped the Lord with expectation, knowing that every life had a purpose and if we made the commitment to tarry in His presence, God would reveal His perfect will not just for the present but for every moment. This had become my norm from the moment that Pastor Charles had entreated the Lord on my behalf. Today was another day that God had allowed me to be alive which meant that the Lord had more in store for my life. I closed out my time of intersession and re-entered the house which felt customarily peaceful. My family knew that when I was at one with God, I liked to be uninterrupted. The joy I felt was incomparable and had literally changed the course of my life.

I had made preparations to go to the church and meet with my Pastor. I took two tickets from my dresser drawer and placed them in my wallet. Apostle Edwards had played a great role in my life in getting me to this place. I closed the door quietly in order to not disturb anyone and made my way to the garage. I was still in awe for the blessing of owning my own car; it definitely gave me a feeling of independence. I was at the church in a few minutes and was met by Pastor Edwards at the entrance. "I thought you'd make it before I headed back to the office" he said with a firm handshake. "I needed to get my briefcase from the car, anyways that's history" he chuckled "so happy you could make it". We stepped into the office and I took the seat that he had pulled out for me. "Well" he continued "are you ready for the big event?" "I can't imagine how excited you must be" he chuckled. "Amen" I agreed "I'm really excited and ready to share with the world the message of Jesus Christ. Sir I just wanted to come here this morning and personally thank you for being a blessing in my life. You gave me the opportunity on blind faith and took me on as a music minister. Today that door has led to this place and I wanted to personally thank you for believing in me". I took the tickets from my wallet and placed them in his hand and thanked him again before leaving the office.

I opened the door at home and was instantly surprised by Ma Anna standing in the living room. I ran toward her, lifted the small woman and spun her gently. I released her and stood back to make sure that my eyes weren't deceiving me. Anna was the happiest I'd ever seen her and hugged me as she sobbed and stroke my face. Mrs. Fraser joined us from the living room and cried out as she entered "got you good, didn't we?" she teased. I smiled and agreed as she filled me in on how they'd change the time of her arrival from tomorrow to this morning after they learnt from Pastor Edwards that I was meeting with him. I hugged Mrs. Fraser and thanked her for making my day even brighter. I was overwhelmed to the point of tears; this was the only mother I knew for most of my like. We held hands and followed the woman of the house as she served us in her usual hospitable manner. There was so much to catch up on so I listened as Ma Anna told me of the transition my father made in the house. He was definitely a changed man; he was also visiting Pastor Donnie's church and the hand of the Lord was evident in his life. She also made mention of my brothers and the changes among my sibling; they were slowly adapting to the change in our dad. We finished our meal but remained at the table and reminisced on the moments that we spent together. Looking back at my life made me aware that God was my provider; He had kept me in my mother's womb and held me ever since. I was aware that the Lord had placed even what seemed to be the smallest detail to be a stepping stone to my blessing. He had provided for me both spiritually and physically; even to the very smooth rock that was my cushion was in the perfect plan of God. The day was now far spent as I waited in my room while the women engaged socially and got even more acquainted to each other. I must have fallen asleep because I was awakened by a faint knock on my door. Elder Mike was standing in the doorway as I opened my eyes; he apologized for the disturbance and reminded me that I had to be back at the venue for a final sound check.

The day had finally arrived for the awards; I rolled out of bed and made my way to the back of the house. I was eager to meet with the Sovereign Lord and worshiped in His presence. I walked to my usual spot and stretched out before the Him. I immediately felt the anointing and lifted my heart in true worship; I wanted nothing more than to enter into the holies of holies. I began to cry as I worshiped the name of Jesus; the worship escalated at every passing moment as I was taken into the most holy place. I began to seek the Lord as my worship was now mixed with prayers of thanksgiving glorifying Him for His grace towards me. How great is His faithfulness I thought, morning by morning new mercies we see; God had thought me the true meaning of life. I was born to worship and once I really understood my purpose I was at peace.

The house was filled with laughter as I re-entered; I wasn't surprised to see Ma Anna and Mrs. Fraser up as they prepared the food for the brunch. Kylee had planned a special day in my honor to celebrate with me before the Stellar Awards. "Hi son" Anna greeted as she heard my footsteps; "are you ready for your big day?" she smiled. "I am but are you?" I teased, "do you think you have enough food?" "It looks like you are expecting an army". "You best be good and go get ready" she scolded, "time waits on no man". She continued to prepare the food as I walked over and kissed her on her cheek and continued to my room. I knew that everyone was expected to be here by 10:00AM which gave me about an hour or so to get prepared. I could hear as the men from the special event store unloaded and arranged the tables and chairs for the brunch. I walked in the shower and prepared myself to join my friends and family for a few hours of food and fellowship. I took a second look in the mirror before heading into the kitchen. Abigail was busy displaying on a silver platter the pastries that were provided by Mala and Majie's Delectables. "Hey brother" she called. I walked over to her and took a cookie from the dish she had in her hands. "Don't go spoiling your appetite" she warned, "they outdid themselves if you should ask me". I agreed and began to assist her as we brought the food to the buffet table that was on the lawn. The yard was gorgeously set up to match the beautiful day. The guests had started to arrive and everyone was in high spirits. Destiny walked in accompanied by her bother Elder Onajhe and her sister Evangelist Ashley. Immediately following was her Godmother, Aunty Paulette and her daughter Ariana. They all took turns to embrace and congratulate me as they took their seat of choice. The Johnson's were next to arrive accompanied by Mrs. Johnson's Senior National director with the prestigious company 'Mary Kay cosmetics', Mrs. Darnette Cohen-Spencer and her beautiful daughter Chanelle. They were the focus upon arrival as they made their appearance in the coveted pink Cadillac. Pastor Edwards took his place at the head table and opened in prayer and the party got officially started. He handed the mike to Elder Michael who blessed the food, thanked his wife and Ma Anna for preparing the meal, and the Johnson's for the authentic mouth-watering dishes. We left our tables as everyone served themselves according to their preference; the day was turning out to be a fantastic one. My CD was playing in the background as the children danced to the music; the handsome twins Jeremiah and Isaiah along with Chase were playfully having a dance off with Keziah and Kayleigh because Kehjon their older cousin promised the winner a large bag of candy. God was in the midst of us and we could feel Him in the atmosphere as we worshipped to each song that serenaded our souls. Kylee took the mike and called us to attention, "praise the Lord" she greeted "I hope you're all having a good time". There was a round of applause and a response of 'amens' as we all agreed. "Well let me be the first to congratulate my brother on his accomplishments". "David" she said, "this is just the first of many more awards; we love and support you beloved". The Mike was handed from one person to the next as they saluted me on my milestone.

I closed the bedroom door and began to undress for the next phase of the day. The women were also busy getting themselves flawless for the event. Mrs. Cohen-Spencer had come prepared to give them a classic makeover; Ma Anna was also a part of the company waiting to receive her services. I turned on the water and began to fill up the tub, 'today I was going to get the treatment fit for a king', I thought to myself. I poured the solution in the tub and waited for it to fill to the appropriate level. I suddenly remembered that there was something on my agenda but for some reason I couldn't put my finger on it. I closed my eyes and began to retract my list of priorities and suddenly the thought came back to me; I needed to call my dad. I picked up the phone from the receiver and dialed his number, "hi son" his voice came through the receiver, "praise the Lord" I responded. "I missed you today" I continued, "but I understood you just weren't able to make it. How are you though?" I continued "I pray all is well" "amen" he answered "I'm doing excellent, actually I am just on my way back to the main house. I was on the back of the property meditating on the goodness of the Lord for a moment". I swallowed hard and suddenly there was a peace that overtook me; the thought of him confiding in me was stupendous. We chatted for a little while and truly it was refreshing to indulge in a conversation of this nature with my father. "Dad" I interrupted his thoughts "I really wish you were here, but the Lord knows all things well" I said and remained quiet. "Amen" he agreed "He knows all things well", he was silent for a moment them continued in a low tone. "I'll be there in spirits and so will your mom" he said in a sincere tone. "Amen daddy' I whispered. "Dad I gotta go, the Limo will be here soon" I said hurriedly. "Ok" he said "I know you have a big night ahead of you but remember that the Lord had predestined this day before the very foundation of the word". "Son" he continued "I'm very proud of your hard work and accomplishments; if anybody deserves to be at this place, it's you". I closed my eyes in order to blink back the streaming tears, then I tried my hardest to sound as cool as possible. "Thanks dad, I really appreciate those words coming from you, I will be in touch" I said and ended the call.

I made my way to the bathroom and as quickly as I could, I stepped into the tub and began to drown out my tears. I knew that my life was exactly where it needed to be at this particular moment, but I couldn't help but wonder what if? I oftentimes wonder how she looked, does she ache for me as I did for her; 'mommy' I heard my heart mourned 'I miss you'. I buried my thoughts in the great moments that life had offered and reflected on all that the Lord had allowed me to accomplish in this year. The souls that were saved was definitely my biggest accomplishment and I was immediately encouraged. The water was losing its warmth and I knew that was an indication that I'd been here long enough. I completed my bath and thanked the Lord for releasing me both physically and emotionally and stepped from the tub. I wrapped the oversized towel around my body and stepped into my room, glancing at the clock and realized that time was now at hand. I began to quicken my pace and with that in mind I reached into my closet removing the classic tuxedo and began the transformation process. I laughed at the thought of the statement from Mr.

J, as he said "this will transform even the most reserved man and give him new confidence". I removed the suit from the bag and began to carefully attire myself; I was amazed at the dramatic transformation the garment contributed to my appearance. I put on the final touches and took a last look at the handsome man looking back at me in the mirror.

There was silence as I walked into the main area; Ma Anna who was more beautiful than ever made her way toward me and took my face in her hands. "Look what you're about to do boy baby; you're going to make Mrs. Cohen-Spencer get upset if I mess up this look". She patted her eyes, smiled and said "baby you are more handsome than ever; look at my son". I smiled as she complimented me over and over. The women were all looking at me in awe and took turns to compliment me. Everyone was picture perfect; Mrs. Cohen-Spencer had done a phenomenal job in accomplishing a natural but flawless look on the ladies. There was a knock on the door which interrupted the combined conversation as the ladies finished their final touches. I excused myself and answered the visitor. I was met by Minister Daniel and Elder Johnson who were equipped with professional photography equipment. Elder Johnson was being his normal self and began to take photos of me unannounced. He was at his peak of excitement as he photographed with utmost professionalism.

Destiny was unusually quiet as she sat beside her bestie Ariana, who was teasing her for being paparazzi. She smiled at me and in that moment I knew what she felt and that really meant a great deal to me. We all completed all of Elder Johnson photographic requirements and exited the house loading into the limousine one after another. Elder Michael led us in prayer before we began our journey, thanking the Lord for keeping us and to take us safely, in Jesus name.

I was amazed at the anointing that was in the building and the fellowship backstage was genuine. Pastor Donnie was the first to greet me; he was convinced that I was going to be the last man standing. The show started and I was stunned at how each artist was humbled to be in this arena and it made me recognize that we were mere servants. The MC for the nights' event was none other than the anointed woman of God CeCe Winans. I was enjoying every moment of the show and was informed that I was scheduled to minister next. I made my way to the stage and the anointing hit me from the top of my head to the very soul of my feet. I began to worship the Lord and the power of God swept the entire audience; I was humbled to have the Lord use me in such a manner. I left the stage giving all honor to He who equips us with great gifts for His glory.

I accidentally brushed the side of a stately looking woman and she looked me in the eye and said "just as I expected my son, I love you". I apologized and quickly regained my composure but she held my hand and said, "I am and will remain your greatest fan". Ma Anna looked at us and smiled then quickly looked away. I told the lady I was blessed to know that I was loved by strangers. In my peripheral view, I saw my dad and my brothers smiling from ear to ear and gave me a thumbs up. I really felt special for the love and support from siblings that I thought disliked me. My dad looked nervously in the direction of the strange lady and immediately began to exit the building. 'Very weird' I thought.

Time was far spent and the categories were announced. The presenters were excited as children as they presented the awards. I was now seated in the audience as I kept my composure and watched in anticipation. I almost fell out of my seat when I heard the MC calling my name. She shouted "for best CD of the year, the award goes to David Manner". Ma Anna and Elder Mike took turns to hug me as I made my way to the stage. I took the award from the presenter and looked up to the Lord, knowing that this was His doing. "I just want to first give honor to the Lord Jesus Christ who is the head of my life. I owe this to my Heavenly Father who entrusted this vision to me. I want to thank a special woman, I call her mama Anna. Please stand so that everyone can see a lady that believed in me from the very beginning; also to a very special family, a man who is a father to me, Mr. Michael Fraser, his wife and daughters. To my brother and sister, Kylee and Daniel and their parents Mr. and Mrs. Johnson. To my collaborator and friend the anointed Destiny James who believed that the Lord was with me from jumpstart. To a man that saw the vision and invested his time and so much more, Pastor Donnie thank you so much. I also want to thank the supporters who made this possible; the word of God is all we need and I see that you guys were appreciative of the gifting, thank you all". I closed out and left the stage as they all stood and applauded, giving the Lord praise. I left that night accomplishing more than I expected, the award went to yours truly in all four categories; it was a night that I would never ever forget. My life was changed and no one will ever see me the same again. I was the official David Manner, a man called to live an exemplary life as a gospel recording artist.

My life was a journey, one filled with much distractions. The enemy had tried to derail the plan of God but was not allowed to do so; I stayed in prayer and most importantly maintained an intimate relationship with God irrespective of the trials. When I look back over my life, I recognize that without faith it's impossible to please God. The mighty hand of God led me in every juncture and the Lord had purposed me for His will. I know that through it all, He had shadowed my every step and kept me in the hollow of His mighty hands; from defeat to victory 'hallelujah'.

Epilogue

I was in total awe of what I'd just experienced. I realized that God had a way of amazing you even at your highest expectation. My thoughts went back to my early days and felt like I was completely alone. The table had completely turned and I was blessed with so many individuals that made a positive impact in my life. The Lord had opened the portals and had blessed my life beyond measure. I was not merely David Manner, but was Minister David Manner that was handpicked by God to serve. The Lord promoted me and also favored me as a rising gospel recording artist that was assigned to change or impact a generation with what was bestowed upon me. I was ready for the challenge knowing that I was fully equipped by the Heavenly Father. Destiny held my hand and whispered, 'penny for your thoughts', I chuckled and looked deep in her eyes and whispered, 'penny for you thoughts'.